Charles Sanford Olmsted

December Musings and Other Poems

Charles Sanford Olmsted

December Musings and Other Poems

ISBN/EAN: 9783744707862

Printed in Europe, USA, Canada, Australia, Japan

Cover: Foto ©Andreas Hilbeck / pixelio.de

More available books at **www.hansebooks.com**

December Musings

and Other Poems

by

Charles Sanford Olmsted

PHILADELPHIA

GEORGE W. JACOBS & CO.

1898

To

Anna Morison Core

and

The Rev. Frank Burrows Reazor, M. A.

A token of respect and affection

CONTENTS

CONTENTS

CONTENTS

CONTENTS

DECEMBER MUSINGS

Introductory

He lay within the deeper shade of death,
And through sequestered rooms there came a
    breath
Of peril and disease, and I, shut in
From human fellowship, no peace could win

From books nor anything; and then these lines
And many hundreds more, like ivy vines
Upon the church walls, grew from out my heart,
And did a shelter from strong woe impart.

December Musings let them now be called,
And let them bless at least some spirits walled
About and weary with the stress of fears—
And so my God shall wipe away their tears.

RECTORY
CHURCH OF ST. ASAPH
BALA, PENNA.
1898

December Musings

Too fast we hasten through the flowery ways
Of life's wide mysteries, as if for praise
And saintly meditation few could find
Those moments when at morn and eve the mind

Might seek refreshment from God's holy works,
In whose interior depths there lives and lurks
A mystic lore.　Each calm neglected hour
We miss some touch of sweetness or of power.

But why this haste?　Our time is lengthened out
For spiritual visions, and our paths about
Are strewn with lessons bright as dewy beads,
When Morning walks among the summer meads.

Our lives are poor when God can make them rich,
His hills rise all about, while in the ditch
We stay to dig, as if we there could see
Some vestige of our immortality.

We toil so hard and lose our recompense,
Begin to learn just when we're taken hence
What treasures passed us by unrecognized,
What gifts and glories that we never prized.

Images of Eternal God are we,
Whose light reveals itself wherein we see
His children pray. Oh, why then should we fret
Our souls away a little earth to get ?

Arise and eat ; behold the ravens come
To bring us food from out no narrow home,
And see the waters clear as crystal flow
From heavenly mountains to the plain below.

The meat to eat that others know not of,
The hidden manna and the cup of love,
The palm-tree and the sweet sequestered well,
All of His tender watchfulness do tell.

Oh, sit thee down and rest, thou hung'ring heart
That through long paths of fatal famine swart
Hast wandered on ; unbind the sandals worn ;
For His white robe exchange these garments torn.

Anoint thy head and wash thy face the while
And let the waters see that thou canst smile ;
Take now no thought of time, but be refreshed,
That with life's trials wast so long enmeshed.

Thy weary cares shall pass so soon away
That they should count e'en now no more than clay
To Him whose ivory palaces outshine
The house of Nero, or of Antonine.

His banner over thee is love, His bowers
Will shelter thee all through the midday hours ;
Across the drowsy desert thou shalt see
The gleaming domes of His eternity.

II

SILENCE unfolds her ancient mysteries
And scatters them like flowers through all the skies ;
The light sheds forth a comfort more serene;
The meadow lands are clothed with richer green;

The waters have foregone their former pride,
And with a simple resignation glide
Slowly along, but wear a purer hue
By stretching waveless to the heavenly blue.

For now has dawned the Lord's own holy day,
And all the world has risen up to pray;
Nature is charmed, and half forgets the while
Her deeper energies, and stops to smile.

The sire's rich voice is laden with a hymn
Answered by robins on the maple's limb;
And softly sounds the solemn distant bell,
Which makes the silence deeper with its spell.

We hear the Scripture, and lift up the heart;
Grandsire and granddame each bears out a part
In Jesus' words and with familiar prayers,
Which take far off their sorrows and their cares.

We hear a hymn now stealing down the hill,
And pass out midst the trees to wait until
It dies away, and then to worship go,
Through sunny paths, with happy steps and slow.

O heavenly is the church on summer morns
Mid rural scenes! How sweetly it adorns
The verdant upland! How its tapering spire
Founded in massive tower and rising higher

Than ancient trees around seems like a road
Soon lost in light, that leads to the abode
Of generations long since gone that way,
And dwelling now within the clearer ray

Of that celestial peace ! They once below
Found sorrow's solace at the altar's glow,
And we by faith, may see th' eternal light
Break into stars, and quench our dreary night.

III

SWEET are the hours of Sunday afternoon
Spent much alone, perchance with blissful boon
Of breeze in some deep dell, and rare old book
Of holy meditation, from which look

With vivid spiritual glance the saints
That did themselves impart to it with plaints
All penitential now, and now with praise,
And utmost-reaching sighs and fervent lays.

To be alone with God at this blest time
By Him made holy, and with light sublime
Of Father, Son and Holy Ghost indued,
Nor let the world, nor time's great wheels intrude;

O this is to be great, this is to bring
Ourselves within the shadow of His wing,
And listen for His silence in the soul,
And read the pages of His secret scroll.

And then to walk along the little stream,
And let the soothéd spirit calmly dream
Unutterable things and see the sky
Rest in the waters, as our God on high

Deep in responsive souls is wont to rest,
And then to see the sun sink in the west,
As life at last sinks to its dear repose—
A truer consolation no man knows.

Then sweet it is to gather at the door
Of consecrated fane, where evermore
The holy voices of dear Christians blest
Seem with the tender glory of the west

To glide away, and evening hymns and psalms
To blend with fragrant flowers and wholesome balms
That through the opened panes are wafted in,
From fields and forests where the day has been ;

And sweet to hear the benedictory tone
From God's pure minister, as in it shone
The light of sacrifice all glowing yet
From boundaries where heaven and earth are met;

And sweet to spend the quiet evening hours
By household hearth, and 'mid the opening flowers
Deep rooted in our deepest heart, whose bloom
Perchance shall lend a comfort to the tomb ;

And sweet to rest in peace with God and man,
And wait His coming when our earthly span
Is measured o'er, and all our work is done,
And find in Jesus all our victory won.

IV

ONE picture ever wins upon my heart :
Love seems to struggle with the painter's art
To make it tell the story of God's grace
To our benighted, weak and slumbering race.

Christ knocks and listens at the sleeper's door ;
His looks are sad and anxious, as He wore
Some pain within : His alb is long and white,
And all adown it falls a tender light

Cast from a lanthorn in His hand, which shines
Upon the door, and down among the vines,
Which climb about, and up along His face,
Creating a mild splendor in the place.

His outer robe is royal: On His head
A crown of thorns He wears as when He bled
On Calvary: with wondrous graciousness
He seems to come to comfort and to bless.

This picture for a score of cycling years
Has hung itself before my mind, and tears
Sometimes give added grace, as through a mist
I saw the tender majesty of Christ.

'Tis thus Thou comest, Lord, for evermore,
Knocking and waiting at the lowly door,
If only we might rise and let Thee in,
And so be fed by Thee and healed of sin.

O when Thou comest once again, good Lord!
And with the lanthorn of Thy sacred word
Sheddest a beam of truth within my breast,
Stay Thou till shadows flee away, and rest!

V

How deep into the heart will strike a blow,
Like a strong arrow from a well-strung bow,
When hymn or song one's mother used to sing
Through door or lattice suddenly will ring!

Oh! then the time seems for a moment gone
Far back into the past, as if alone
One sat by her beside the cheerful hearth,
And nothing knew of evil in the earth.

And once again one sees the tender face
With lines and features of refinéd grace,
In which a man's mature analysis
Discovers all its light of saintly bliss.

And once again one feels those radiant hours
When home returning to her filial flowers,
With all her nature rich she would rejoice,
Thrilled with the music of her children's voice.

Ah! happy childhood! would that you could know
What treasures you possess before they go
So far away into those silent lands!
From which unseen they stretch their happy hands!

Would that you knew how beautiful they are,
With that maternal beauty which they wear
Along their smiling cheeks, and in those eyes
That gladden with their life of sacrifice!

'Tis only in some sacred silent hour
Long after that, there comes to us with power
Remembrance of their gentle patient ways,
And love unspeakable in olden days.

And they remember us while there they wait
To welcome us within the unbarred gate,
And hope and trust and pray that all is well
With souls for whom their tears so often fell.

And we remember them, oh! heart, be brave,
He who saves them will their's with glory save.
With grace He will thy aspirations cherish,
The child of many prayers shall never perish!

VI

TIME ministers to forgetfulness,
And happy are we that the more or less
Of sorrow in our past fades out of view,
As stormy clouds pass out of heaven's blue.

DECEMBER MUSINGS

If some great joy stand out upon our life,
And some great grief survive the dreadful strife,
We often draw new pleasure from the joy,
And slightly with the grief our thoughts employ.

Within the true and real joys we had
Still do we find new things to make us glad,
And see how kind our Heavenly Father is
To turn old fountains to perennial bliss.

A father's care, a mother's constant love
Will brighten for us long, although above
In other realms they shine, and friendships kind
Will cheer, though friends themselves to us are blind.

Sermons and books and voices of the past
We love and cherish more than all the last
That come confusédly across our way,
Mingling great thoughts with trifles of a day.

When traveling with our faces looking back
The higher landscape seems upon our track
To hasten as the lower falls away
And fades upon our sight to formless gray.

So on our minds the nobler, better things
Loom in their grandeur, as on purple wings;
But tame and toneless shadows of the time
Pass out of life, and leave the world sublime.

VII

A PURPLE cloud draped in a golden mist
Stooped down to Ocean's brow, and gently kist
His whitened locks, and looked in his soft eyes,
Wondering that such angers should arise.

To-morrow will that cloud be far away,
And Ocean will be up at dawn of day
Spending his arrows at the morning sun,
And girding up his loins to leap and run

Before his chariot; he'll catch the beams
That from its axle fly, and swift as streams
That roll down mountain sides he'll onward rush
Singing and shouting with a rapturous blush.

Eternal youth lurks in the Ocean's heart,
The centuries as they pass cannot impart
To his deep lusty life their long decay,
Though he so oft reflect their image gray.

And that unbounded life that waits us there,
Above the weakness, sinfulness and care
Of all this world, glows with a Godlike strength,
Pulsing with joy in depth and breadth and length.

VIII

In slumbrous moments by the open fire,
When tongues of flame seem like the soul's desire
For things above, and in the twilight hour
Illumine faces on the walls with power,

And bring the past again and waken hope,
And golden doors upon the future ope;
What bliss it is, if mingling with half-thought,
A low, soft, distant strain by him is caught,

Who sits and muses, wondering at all things,
And vaguely hoping that the one who sings
Is not a thing of earth and time, but sails
Down avenues of rosy light, that pales

And brightens oft with subtle inward change,
And brings high messages so sweet and strange
And full of dim and solemn mystery,
Like songs of gladness in eternity!

IX

DIM starlit waters overhung with trees
On either bank dwell in the memories
Of life within my brain. Oft would I glide
Wherever I was carried by the tide,

And let the dark mysterious shadows sink
In my deep soul, and feel the bonds that link
Us to the world unseen, in wonder lost
And awe, but in a pleasing sadness most.

What solemn bliss attends the thought of death,
Death that is good and Christian, when the breath
Is laden with the fragrance of a prayer
And goes to mingle with a freer air!

How calm is death, when we have drifted past
The world's high towers, and find ourselves at last
Out where mild glories of the milky way
Seem like the path to our immortal day!

How sweet is death when all our work is done,
And holy darkness separates each one
From all but God! for 'tis the light removes
Those barriers the pensive spirit loves.

How kind is death which comes to give release
To souls long waiting for the endless peace,
Who here knew little but cold wintry rains
And hailstones rattling on the window panes !

How fair is death that calls us in the breeze,
Soft as the murmur of the summer seas,
And guides our bark beyond the freshening tide
Out where the calm, great ocean glimmers wide !

How merciful is death that calms our fears,
And, if we shed them, wipes away our tears ;
And though the billows rise and round us break,
Keeps us within the rising moon's white wake !

How beautiful is death that o'er us bends
To sooth the drooping spirit when it lends
Itself to dreamless languors, and the swoon
Which at the haven will be ended soon !

X

As those who suffer through the winter time
Will think with longing of some milder clime,
Where gentle airs are not afraid to play
Among white roses which adorn the way.

So do our wistful spirits often long
To see the country of perpetual song,
Where pain is not and sorrow is unknown,
Where peace and spring-like summer reign alone.

Beyond our vision lies the heavenly realm,
The hope of seeing which will overwhelm
Us often with unconquerable joy,
And with some rapturous song our tongues employ.

How could we live among these earthly scenes,
Fair as they are, and always gracious means
Of echoing things beyond, if they could last,
And those fade out, as visions of the past.

As shadows of the things which shall endure,
Invincible and everlasting : pure
As morning on the hills, how dear they are,
Clear and bright images of things afar!

But oh! the substance—heavenly things themselves—
In whose vast depths the unsphered spirit delves
For hidden glories of eternal mind,
As new to us as colors to the blind!

A little while, a few more days below,
And on our eyes shall open all the glow
And gladness of those ever-shining lands,
Where spirits beckon with their happy hands.

The moments vanish, but the ages wait:
Time kindly brings us to th' eternal gate :
The Saviour comes, He does not tarry long,
Our sighs shall melt forever into song !

Like shadows of the little moonlit flowers
Upon the grass we live our mortal hours ;
Like dewdrops caught up by the morning sun
To our Creator's arms we quickly run.

In dying we shall throw across the grave
A shadow like a bird's upon the wave;
O'er which with quivering wing she flies
To sing her bright song in the morning skies.

Like billows fleeting o'er the aged sea
So are our years in God's eternity ;
They pass away but that shall still endure,
Life passes, but the longer life is sure !

XI

WHO has not felt the pressure of a power
Unseen, when at the solemn twilight hour
He stood within some ancient fane most fair,
And saw the blended gloom and glory there?

Through lofty painted windows overhead
The last great beams of daylight softly spread
Across the silent walls, and filtered down
Through arches dim like moonlight in the town.

Who did not linger lost in reverie,
To see the halos fade and every
Saintly form grow dim, and long shafts of light
Grow fainter, in the heavy grasp of night.

So some do linger here till very late
To watch Day's final flight, and calmly wait
Where shadows melt in shadows, and the bloom
Of evening passes into hueless gloom.

So waited the beloved John, who sate
Far into night, surviving every mate
With whom he kept the glorious paschal feast,
And saw his master act as Great High Priest.

Our times are in God's hands ; then gladly rest
We still where still He makes us daily blest
With love and gentleness, and as our days
So shall our strength be, and our thankful lays.

XII

I SAW long since a picture sweet and fair,
A flight of angels rising through the air
From out a church tower when the sunset glow
Fell on the fields, and filled the vales below.

I praised the artist's gift, and loved his thought ;
And often has the picture deeply wrought
Within my heart, and made me long to reach
All that so wonderful a stroke might teach.

Angels are with us in our worship here,
Filling our poor notes with a heavenly cheer,
And taking with them echoes of our song,
Ere shadows fall upon us all night long.

And as the angels from the sacred tower
Rise unto heavenly places at that hour,
So shall we pass before the deeper night
Shuts out the sunset hues so rich and bright

Angels of sunset! at our evensong
Sing with us ever, and enrich our tongue,
And take us with you when our final hymn
Dies 'midst the chancel and the arches dim.

XIII

SAINT FRANCIS, in his sickness languishing,
Beholds an angel sent from heaven to sing
His ills away, as some fine legend tells,
Like Saul relieved by David in his spells.

Ignatius, so another legend speaks,
Preserves the music which from heaven breaks,
And sets it to the anthem sung in choir,
And so all Antioch feels the awful fire.

Sweet voices haunt us from the realms above,
Revealing to us all-surpassing love;
And if we only listen and obey
Our sorrows and our fears flit fast away.

So if in memory we keep the song
That smites our souls with love, and makes us long
For greater gifts and richer blooms of grace,
We shall be helpers of our sin-worn race.

XIV

SAINT IMIER at midnight in his cell
Hears ringing clear the monastery bell
That is to be ; and, guided by the sound,
Like Abram seeks his consecrated ground.

And so we in our simple hermitage
Of prayer may hear alike in youth and age
The call ring out from future rhythmic years,
And follow till our destiny appears.

For here we walk by faith and not by sight,
We go through darkness to the land of light ;
We go through toil our recompense to gain,
And by submission perfectness attain.

Slowly but surely we are hastening on,
Soon will Time's precious moments all be gone ;
O let us fill our hearts with heavenly light
While here we may, against the coming night !

XV

'TIS very late, and many a weary mile
I've journeyed on : I come to knock the while
Upon the door ; and must I stand here long ?
But now within I hear their evensong.

One comes to listen, and my voice is known ;
The steps retire : and am I left alone ?
For gladness they could not unbar the gate,
But now they come : I shall not have to wait.

'Tis late, 'tis very late, but oh ! how rare
My welcome is in this sweet home of prayer;
God's children seek me with their kindly eyes,
And I sit down among the good and wise !

'Tis late, 'tis very late : but tarry not
Ye who are laboring in your heavy lot,
Follow your guide and you shall find your rest,
And be among the happy happiest guest !

XVI

FAREWELL to death ! such is the victor song
Of those who walk th' immortal fields among :
Men only once can die, and these have died—
What happiness they share at Jesus' side !

Farewell to death ! oh, what a lot is theirs
Henceforth to look for life alone : the heirs
Of all that life in all its richness holds,
Beholders rapt of joys it aye unfolds.

Farewell to death ! and these were mortals born,
Who all their lives the yoke of death had worn,
Subjects of pain and weariness and sin,
Who now at last so great a conquest win.

Farewell to death ! and shall this be our song,
Who to these lowly vales of earth belong ?
Our Saviour Christ the answer can supply,
Sons of the resurrection no more die.

Farewell to death ! O this shall be our theme
When the vast world with living forms shall teem ;
Like incense shall arise our earliest breath,
Among its burdens this, farewell to death !

XVII

WITH windows open toward Jerusalem,
Devout, unmindful of all human blame,
A man of God in ancient Babylon
Through daily prayer celestial wisdom won.

Unless we let the light and sweetness in,
That flow like rivers to this world of sin
From heavenly founts, our labored prayers are vain :
They leave us like a desert after rain,

Fruitless as ever; feverish to the heart,
Unreached, unblessed, unbettered e'en in part:
Such prayers, as smoke that breaks not into flame
Consumes no chaff, no lasting blessing claim.

XVIII

REPENTANCE from past sin will not efface
All its ill consequence, nor e'en the trace
Of its own sorrow, though true pardon bring
New peace and comfort on its silver wing.

Lo! when God brought His ancient people home
From Babylon, that they should no more roam,
Nor idols seek, the temple's golden shields
Were not restored to grace their olden fields.

Not here, not here can exiles find again
The sinless joys which they themselves have slain;
They only can recover every gem
When they arrive at New Jerusalem.

XIX

A CUSTOM lingers from the Celtic times
To bury where the bells or glorious chimes
Ring in the people to the house of prayer,
And turn to music all the happy air.

Anear the doors, along the sacred walls,
Within the aisles, and chancel dim there falls
On grave and tomb the shadow of the fane,
Or light that streams from some rich window pane.

And they who slowly walk among the graves
And kneel within the ancient lofty naves,
Will soon among those ling'ring shadows seek
Their long still rest, and to the future speak

As speaks the past to them, and like the old
Great prophet of the Hebrew race grow cold
Only to gain new life, through memories sweet
To those who touch them with their passing feet.

How lovely is the fellowship of saints!
No poet sings nor sacred prophet paints
Its tender grace, its golden atmosphere,
Its melodies that fall upon the ear.

Living and dead within one circle meet;
The gentle shadow and rich sunshine greet
All that are gathered where the sound of grace
Rings out to gladden Christ's redeeméd race.

Distance is not : from earth to paradise
Is like the step from church out where the skies
Pour down incessant shafts of quick'ning light,
Filled with a message from the Infinite.

XX

THERE is a picture of Teutonic tone,
Wrought by a pencil dipped where softly shone
The hues of homelike sanctity ! it seems
A holy temple full of heavenly dreams.

It is a gathered family at prayer ;
The faces mildly shine as if the air
Were interfused with indefinable
And tender quiv'ring gleams, which gently quell

The shadow cast by care and daily toil ;
Or as anointed by a hallowing oil
From inner shrines brought out, such restfulness
And such calm eager joy do there express

Themselves. The father reads from that dear book,
Wherein God's face will answer to our look,
And by him stands his boy of six or seven
Like some sweet little cherub sent from heaven.

Over against them sits the youthful wife,
Whose conscious thoughts are on the Word of Life,
But whose unconscious wait upon the child
In arms, all wrapped in slumbers undefiled.

By her the grandsire's widow forward leans
Upon her staff, and with devotion gleans
What grace or mercy falls upon her ear,
By kind accustomed tones made doubly dear.

A girl of twelve stands well behind her chair,
Yet so as of her father's face to share
Her portion, as its native kindliness
Is lighted with the words that soothe and bless.

One other form there is by them unseen,
Standing in white within a misty sheen,
With hands outstretched in blessings o'er their heads,
As when on mountain tops the morning spreads.

'Tis Jesus, who in lowly Nazareth
Obedient lived, as Holy Scripture saith ;
And by experience of our living found
How rare and sacred is the household bound.

A glory burns upon a Christian hearth,
Brighter than all the glories of the earth,
When through the morning and the evening air
The voice uprises of united prayer.

For God who sits between the cherubim
Descends in fragrant cloud when holy hymn
And prayer go up from gracious simple hearts,
And all His love and favor He imparts.

'Tis He who sets mankind in families,
And loves to train them like the fruitful trees
In beauteous growth, and keep them pure and sweet,
That evermore at cool of day His feet

May walk among them and His voice be heard
Speaking so gloriously through His word,
And pardon bring, and peace, and holy light
To comfort them all through the darksome night.

XXI

EGYPTIAN wagons made old Israel faint ;
And now the chariot of the famished saint
Awaits him at his tent ; he tarries not ;
The fairest provinces fall to his lot

In regions where the ministering Son
Lives in His regal might to bless each one
Whose flesh He wears, with corn and wine and oil,
Such as were never seen on earthly soil.

We seek for sustenance among the stores
Of riches manifold, and from these shores
O let us take the best fruits of our lands !
Be sure He will accept them at our hands.

A little balm and honey, spice and myrrh,
Almonds and nuts, such it sufficient were
To show our fealty and fruitfulness ;
For all our living we could take no less.

He freely gives us everlasting bread,
Himself He gives, who is our royal Head ;
'Tis very little we can find to bring
To be the semblance of an offering.

Among the scanty remnants of our waste
Perchance we may pick up amid our haste
A tribute to His honor whom we trust,
Who raises us to kingdoms from the dust.

The good of all that land is surely ours;
'Twill be all bright and blossomy with flowers;
'Twill shine with rivers of serene delight,
And all its priestly children walk in white;

And all are crowned with radiant crowns of gold;
And all move to the chant of ages old
Before sin entered our sad world so dim,
And changed the keynote of our daily hymn.

XXII

MOSES wist not his countenance did shine
When from communion high with the Divine
To Israel's tents he came; souls deep and great
Drawn upward, look beyond the gate,

And lost in wonder at the glorious sight
Of that most fair and uncreated light,
Wherein all truth and mercy ever met,
Forget the world, and e'en themselves forget.

The sight of God we have by faith upholds
Our weary steps, and day by day unfolds
Such peace as all the world can never give,
And so great joy as makes it joy to live.

It is our truest happiness to fade
From self away, and in the restful shade
Of God's eternal throne to stay awhile,
Like John in vision in the sacred isle :

To climb to mountain heights amid the gloom,
And find within a purer light, and room
To open richer treasures of His grace,
And count those stars which do not shine in space;

To get beyond, and into silence come,
And meet with God alone, and there be dumb;
While He makes all His goodness pass us by,
Like pearly clouds upon the summer sky.

O then we see fair Mercy like a bow
Of promise stretching wide her arms, aglow
With tearful light, her eyes shine wondrously
As full of blessing as the boundless sky.

And then we hear proclaimed the awful name
Of God's Almightiness, and lo ! the flame
Descends from His pure altar, downward drawn
Like sunbeams when the sun looks forth at dawn,

And lights upon our hearts, and eats up there
All that is inconsistent with our prayer
To be like Him : and creeps within the door,
And makes that cheerful that was dark before.

Amid the shining stillness of the time
We hear such soft, harmonious, tuneful chime
Far in the heavenly deeps as wounds our ears
With sweetness, and awakens holy tears ;

And makes us wonder if our mortal sense
Is not immortal made, and if from thence
We ever need return to earth again,
To walk with sorrow and sit down with pain,

As if perchance like patriarchs of old,
We have undying come within the fold
And border of the vast eternal sphere,
And sight, not faith, has made it all so clear !

'Tis good for us, kind Master, to be here,
To taste the hidden manna without fear ;
From glory change to glory in Thy sight,
And gaze upon Thy riches infinite.

'Tis good to grow like Thee in silent prayer,
And daily drink this sweet and heavenly air,
And glide along still contemplation's stream,
And see all heaven lie near us like a dream !

Salamis

THE battle day of Salamis was born
Euripides, and Aeschylus that morn
Fought well, and at the feast great Sophocles
Danced to the rhythm of the sounding seas.

Autumn

I

HAIL! Friend and Sister! Clad in russet gold,
With orange coronet upon thy head,
On scented leaves in woodlands will we tread
Together, while they break, and skies unfold
A keener breath, and all the trees, or old
Or young, and bush and hedge, will grow all red
And yellowy-green : with fruits we shall be fed,
When on the hills the vines are overrolled
With purple hues, and when the chilly eve
Falls on the fields, with quickened pace we too
Shall walk, while o'er the western mountain blue
The crimson glories spread, and downward cleave
The passes with long golden swords that sweep
Through paths wherein the shadows soon must creep.

II

THOU walkest through the land all silently,
Autumnal shade! Yet in thy footsteps leav'st
A hue of deeper tone : and where thou cleav'st
The forests with thy frosty breath they sigh,
And shed their foliage on the earth to die.
I wonder if thou ever fondly griev'st
When from the hills and vales thou gently reav'st

Their silvery beauty, soft and summery!
Dear wondrous daughter of the changing skies!
Thou teachest us how all things mortal fade,
But also this—that something beautifies
The passage to the grave, and that the shade
Of Death puts on its sunset hues when flies
The spirit home, weary but unafraid.

III

THY ripening touch is on the harvest field,
Thy smile austere yet kind is in the sky,
And glory follows in thy path. On high
Thou flingest forth thy banners, and thy shield
Of every leaf is wrought. Now thou dost wield
The sickle and the axe—thy weapons bright—
And closest in the day with earlier night,
So thou canst sit with us, and gently yield
By fireside and the lamp—true learning's friend—
Such stores of wisdom, all mature and sweet,
As have been trodden out by patient feet
In threshing-floors of Pallas. Thou dost send
The poet joy and utmost-reaching vision,
And purple foregleams of the land Elysian.

IV

BELOVED Autumn! How I love thy face!
Thou art to me more beautiful than spring,
Though when thou stayest birds unfold the wing
And fly afar. Thou hast a charm and grace
Which summer, with its silent loveliness
Doth not exceed. In thy soft hazel eyes
There are such beauties and such sympathies
As spring's great blue and summer's black ne'er
    trace
Upon the heart, nor sink within its deep
And wonderful abyss. In thy fair hands
Are bounties not less rare than those which steep
Spring's fingers in a fragrance such as lands
Arabian breathe from spicy fields; and on thy brown
Locks tinged with gold there lies a topaz crown.

V

SWEET Autumn! What deep tenderness is thine!
What kindly tones are in thy voice! What calm
Tranquility adorns thy brow! The balm
Of harvests and the blossoms of the vine
Make thee delightful. Now the sun doth shine
With beam more golden than the gold that rings
Thy vesture, flowing wide. Pure opal springs

Break in the depths far underneath divine
And lustrous streams.   Within the wood thy spell
Makes points of ruddy light where erst the green
And shaded deeps with tender mossy sheen
Were bathed, and soft and dewy languors.   Well
Hast thou given us from thy abundant store,
And into Nature's heart hast oped thy door.

VI

RUBY and topaz and bright gold with rich
Abundance shine out here and everywhere ;
By Nature's alchemy changed from the fair
Emeralds and sapphires and silver, which
In springlike summer field and hedge and ditch
And every hill and vale put on.   The breeze,
So full of melancholy in the trees,
Might make us think a charitable witch,
Or fairy born to deeds of wizardry,
Had climbed the boughs, and in a wondering
Ecstasy how such beauty she could bring
To pass let fall some tears, and gave a sigh
Like that of mortals weak, remembering
How soon created things must fade and die.

VII

ALL this must fade indeed, and quickly die:
Would it could last awhile in all its wealth!
And if we could catch Nature now by stealth
Perchance she might be willing to sit by,
And let this wondrous robe unchangéd lie
About her mighty limbs: but mortals lost
Their grasp long ages since, and now at most
Can only lengthen out the seasons' joy, or fly
To other climes with it, by melodies
That dip themselves in dreams upon the hills,
And in the visions of the golden rills,
And fondly echo soft ethereal sighs.
Dear world! to me thou art forever fair,
And every stole I love that thou dost wear.

Sunset

O SUNSET splendors! flying far I see
A bird that your most sacred depths explores
On wings that doubtless catch a light from doors
Wide opening in you.   How grandly free
It sails upon the crystal air! I flee
With it to you, and on your roseate shores
Would sit, while over me the glory pours
From fountains of the sky.   Eternity
Seems drawing near.   What molten mountains fling
These purple shadows everywhere! My soul
Like that lone bird grows faint with joy: on wing
Of holier song it soars, and in the goal
Of tender beatific light is lost,
Bathed in the wonders of that golden coast.

Subtle Music

ALL, all day long some subtle music haunts
My soul that strives to catch and hold it fast ;
It comes in shadowy breathings: as if past
O'er folded waves in great calm seas, it chants
Remembrance of their song.   For utterance
I sigh.   O could I but reduce the vast
Melodious tone to shape, so it would last
In other ears, and all the world entrance
With pure unshadowed sweetness, I would crown
Myself with bays ! but still alone, alone
I listen, listen, listen, till the frown
Attentive deeply ploughs my brow, and groan
Responsive rises from my breast, and down
In caverns of the heart still echoes moan.

Influence of Beauty

THE air is tender with the unshed rain :
Sunlight is softened by the clouds that roll
More swiftly now across the sky. My soul
Feels the mysterious influence again
Of Beauty, as her fair and fadeless wain
Goes slowly by. O that I might ascend,
And sit beside her in her journey, lend
To her my voice, while she makes ever plain
Her sweet interpretation of all things,
And teaches me her ancient lore ! Ah ! Then
Should I not dwell where everything has wings,
Glide with the stars, and reach abysses when
They echo what the host immortal sings :
And visit only true and righteous men ?

A Pearly Cloud Imparadised in Meads

A PEARLY cloud imparadised in meads
Of boundless ether floats before my eyes,
With which my lonely soul doth sympathize,
Until I wonder whither it must needs
Be carried far of winds; what flowers or weeds
At last it shall descend to bless in drops
Innumerous as weary tears when stops
Some heart-beat here; what ancient upploughed seeds
It will revive and nourish in some place
Unknown to me.   Bright mist! I would that thou
Might'st stay awhile a veil upon the brow
Of Day, a dimple in its guileless face.
But thou dost change and pass, and so must I ;
We both are like the waves that gleam and die.

Ye Tears and Smiles of Holy Infancy

YE tears and smiles of holy infancy !
How do ye mingle and together shine
Within the tender face, and make divine
The lovely child !   My heart beats full and high
When in the sunlight bathed I see the shy
And shrinking baby play, and glance incline
Toward me ; and if I seem to see her fine
Clear eyes, how quickly does she look awry
With head cast down, and lips all pouting red,
Fit for a saint to kiss amid the bright
Calm meadows of the lofty world.   The sight
Is full of heaven ; and round the little head
Winged blessings move invisibly, while Day
Shines softlier whene'er she tunes her lay.

Longings

I

OH ! for long languorous days in which to dream
On solitary hillsides, in the dim
Green light of forests where interfluous hymn
Of birds pure-throated rises in a stream
Of tender melody to heaven ; and deem
All needless but a little beechen bowl
For waters found beneath a grassy knoll,
And fruits and berries plucked where meadows teem
With nature's bounties ; naught should me perturb
Of earth's vicissitude.   I should give way
To wingéd fancy all the golden day,
To roam among the clouds and bright suburb
Of that dear city where the glorious King
Sheds blessings from His eyes on everything.

II

OH ! for long twilights, when the meadows grow
So slowly greener, and the solemn trees
Shut up their stores of twinkles from the breeze :
And mountains in the rapturous distance glow
In light's last purple splendors as they flow
Athwart the world from surge of golden seas,
And Day's bright cohort o'er the horizon flees

To tents of royal hue.   My heart beats so
With love's delight that I could hourly sit
Alone and think and dream and fondly gaze
Far into visions rising from the haze
That weaves its shadowy worlds when sunbeams flit.
Ah! Then if I should hear sweet Music's voice,
With what deep tenderness would I rejoice!

III

OH! for my books when comes the earnest rain
To beautify and brighten all the scene
And tone the field and forest to a green
More rich and deep.   Then near the window pane
I fain would sit and read and look again
Far off across the dimmed and mist-wreathed sky,
For then the sense of freshness seems to lie
Among the visions of the past: a strain
Of Nature's melody with Tasso's song
Is blent, and then how soft o'er deserts spread
The voices of the steel-clad knights that long
Have toiled to reach Jerusalem! the dead
Revive and feel the rushing of the wind,
And from their breasts ruddier streams unbind.

IV

OH! for my friends when cold the night outside
When on the sacred hearth the fire burns bright
And curtains all are drawn.   Far into night
We well may sit and let the tempests ride
Upon the hills.   Here in these gleams we hide
Our cares, and let them rush with quivering tongues
Up into darkness, while we sing our songs
And laugh with generous mirth, and oft confide
One to another our last verse or hope
New-fledged, and let the brighter future ope
Its visions not all futile.   So we share
Earth's kindliness, and if all friends be wise,
Some heavenly joy, some visions still more fair,
Some holier, deeper thoughts and sympathies.

V

OH! for some friends more dear than all the rest,
Sometimes on Sunday evenings it may be,
When tired with much emotion, and set free
From labors that exhaust though always blest,
With whom o'er gentle hills that front the West
We may walk slowly, talk or softly sing,
Or silence keep like birds upon the wing ;

And seat ourselves upon some flowery crest
That overlooks a stream ; perchance the sea,
Spreading its rosy width of mystery
Before our raptured gaze : and then beneath
The starry beams to saunter home and find
Dear faces waiting, lit with love and faith,
Of those who study how they may be kind.

VI

OH! for an old-age far among the hills,
Where in the distance rise the purple peaks
Glistening with jeweled light when Morning breaks
Above, or Evening with her glory fills
The earth and sky.   I want to see the rills
Run down the verdant slopes like silver streaks
Quickened to stronger currents, where the freaks
Of ancient storms left rocks strewn like the ills
That often impulse give to character
In human life.   I want to read again
Mid solitary musings, those old, rare
And precious books, which for long years have lain
Untouched, and then fade out all unaware,
Softly as some calm evening, without pain.

VII

OH ! for a death most Christian and most free
From fears and faithless thoughts.   If I could choose
In perfect resignation how to loose
My shallop from these shores, then I would be
Most willing that the great eternity
Should almost unperceived bear me away,
And angels from the realms of fadeless day
Unfurl my sails and steer me o'er the sea;
While I should think of nothing else but this—
That I shall be all-holy in the bliss
Of God's own company: and learn to tune
My lyre to their sweet voices while I pass.
Then I may duly hymn His praise so soon
As ever I shall reach the sea of glass.

Monastic Life

I

WHAT if the fact oft fall below the aim,
Doth that debase the aim ? No one can take
From Monachism its righteous praise, and make
Its glory fade by pointing to what blame
May blur the beauty of its outward frame.
All things divine put on imperfectness
When they put on a human robe, confess
A human mission, use the weak and lame
For ministers. This wondrous institute
Not more than others failed to work always
A perfect work, yet to its work more praise
Than blame we must accord. An absolute
Devotion reigned within a thousand cells,
And answered gladly to the service bells.

II

As architecture had its lowly birth
In caves, so from the lone, dim hermitage
The monastery sprang. Where simooms rage
And sands Arabian erase from earth
The sandal's print, and in mysterious mirth
The Lybian winds oft chant melodious song,
The silent solitary soul, by wrong

Oppressed, or weak through spiritual dearth,
Prepared its bower among the friendly birds
And kindly beasts : the solemn multitude
Thus driven from the world turned deserts rude
To cities : hermits, joined like gentle herds,
In common lived, and holy minsters rose
By lonely streams, and halls of sweet repose.

III

TEN times ten thousand solitary men
When Athanasius lived in Egypt, toiled
For earthly and for heavenly bread, and foiled
Satanic guile.   Europe the fever then
Received as that high saint and citizen
Of light came into Italy.   From place
To place the marvel spread.   The very face
Of Nature smiled as hill and plain and fen
Felt friendly hands caress their kindred soil.
The happy rivers glassed the lofty towers
That from their banks rose steep, and myriad flowers
Bloomed in the gardens blessed by daily toil :
While gentle beeves fed on the grassy lea,
And long green hillsides sloping to the sea.

IV

IN wondrous vigor for a thousand years
Endured the eremitic institute
In East and West, nor are the echoes mute
Which from the happy hills and vales one hears
Of psalmody all sung with lowly tears
By men escaped from every worldly care.
It is a memory bright—a vision fair,
Which in the Christian centuries appears
From Benedict to Bernard, and from him
To saints no less revered.   I love to trace
The course of Learning's stream in gentle pace
Among the towers and through the arches dim
Of its great homes ; and I do venerate
Its ancient ruins, sad and desolate !

V

A THOUSAND years the Benedictine rule
Made Europe vocal with perpetual praise,
And changed its trackless forests into ways
Of cheerful beauty.   Gates all merciful
Stood open to the poor, the happy school
Of song and science welcomed callow youth,
And daily taught the knowledge of the truth.

Against the world-power, blind and masterful,
Stood out this witness of the Living God
And His pure law, and made barbarian kings
Bow down to spiritual might.   The things
Of heaven put on this guise, and here the road
To peace was found.   Religion's holy light
Upon this beacon cheered the world's dark night.

VI

A THOUSAND years passed tenderly ; great spires
Arose, and minsters glorious with art,
And glorified with lavish love.   The heart
Is pleased as with the sound of sweetest lyres
When strikes this vision home.   The white robed
      choirs,
The altars gleaming with uncounted gems,
And roofs half hid in gloom, the diadems
Of light in pictured panes like lambent fires
That edge the Seraph's purple wings, the dim
Far stretches of the woven light and shade,
The banners by the viewless breezes swayed
Along illuminated walls, the hymn
That swells through aisles and dies with sobs divine,
Make up a picture rich as monk's old wine.

VII

A THOUSAND years the Western world took on
The Christian vow from missioners that moved
Their light from race to race, and bravely roved
Through regions inaccessible. The throne
Reared on Rome's ruins dared to own
The yoke of Christ. Columba from his isle
Breathed peace across the wave, and in the smile
Of Boniface the Frisians saw the blown
Flower of heavenly sanctitude. O Anschar!
Denmark owes her joy to thee: and thou, Gall!
Art honored still in Switzerland, where fall
For ever over hill and dale afar
The bells of thy abode still consecrate,
Where on their offices the brethren wait.

VIII

A THOUSAND years the greatest names were writ
Upon its registers. Great kings and queens
And nobles, worn with war and care, the scenes
Of restful beauty sought, where night was lit
As well as day by prayer's pure flame. Men quit
The noisy world to study God and self,
And triumphed o'er the love of fame and pelf;

In vast dim solitudes embalmed their wit
In myriad tomes, now lost from time's frail
Memory. Basil, Leo, Gregory,
Augustine—son of immortality—
Great Chrysostom, and others time would fail
To tell, that bless the ages, in the halls
Monastic kept angelic festivals.

IX

A THOUSAND years the rising kingdoms basked
In Christian light, shed from its countless towers,
And law and liberty put forth their powers
Under its tutelage. Calm souls were tasked
With peaceful embassies, who fearless asked
For pity on their foes from ruthless knights,
And barons proud as Lucifer. The heights
Of philosophic thought were scaled : and masked
In Christian phrase were Aristotle's lore
And Plato's dreams : and gentle History's self
Piled up new treasures on the shielded shelf,
And even Poesy that laid the floor
And reared the pinnacle, dared to indite
Some faltering lines when stars begemmed the night.

X

FAITH and devotion always lovely are
Wherever found, and in whatever dress
They do their sacred work of righteousness.
These shone upon the world when angry war
Harried the lands—a spiritual star
Set in the Church's firmament, and raised
Men's wearied hearts above the lurid, crazed
And wasted scenes of human life.   Afar
In heaven they lifted up the banner bright
Of Him who fought and won, and led men on
To seek their safety near the Saviour's throne ;
Where evermore came up, both day and night,
A voice of longing for a nobler life,
Untroubled by the sounds of sordid strife !

XI

As one walks through the Evening's thick'ning gloom
The lamps that from the distant windows shine
Seem dots of ineffectual light, divine
Indeed in loveliness, but without bloom
Of radiance ; but near by they assume
Another view.   Far out upon the night
They shed their grateful beam and glimmer quite

Adown the path to welcome pilgrims home.
Through long dim ages as through mountain glens
We see the Monastery's torches gleam,
And peradventure think they were a dream;
But drawing near we find a light that kens
The wilderness, and guides the wanderer
To rest and consolation kind and dear!

Egypt

I

LAND of graves and death, thyself art buried
Half in the sad and dim Lethean stream,
Which like thine own dark river as a dream
Rolls over thee! what wondrous treasures hid
In undiscovered tombs we wait, amid
These latest years of this, Time's latest age!
What strange additions to the heritage
Of this world's past are knocking at the lid
That long has kept them coffined in thy soil,
Now ploughed by many learned hopes! Egypt!
Thou art the world-cathedral's mighty crypt
All rich as treasure-cities built by toil
Of Hebrew slaves. O land of pyramids!
Thy mournful caves my ling'ring fancy thrids.

II

O LAND of fears and shadows! could the shine
Of sun bring mystic glooms upon thy soul,
A shine that deepens as a burning coal
Under the bellows, when upon the vine
And palm it throws itself? Thou art a mine
Of carven gold, and royal forms lie low
Beneath thy languid meads. My heart will grow

Sad ever when to thee my thoughts incline.
Ne'er can I love thee, nor can wish to see
Thy ruined Thebes and Memphis : yet to me
A fascination dwells in thy great past,
As if some witchcraft sceptered it o'er thee
E'en now, and put a spell upon thy vast
Grim relics, awful like eternity.

The Nile

O MOTHER of fertility ! Great Nile !
That sweepest onward like a magic dream,
No tributary ever mingled with thy stream
Of solitary glory.   Many a mile
Thy course is shadowed by majestic pile
Of temples, and the solemn groves of stone,
Where now odd birds make melancholy moan
Like spirits of thine awful past.   The while
I think of thee I seem to see a mist
Breathe from thy depths, peopled with phantoms dire,
And towered cities sunk long since in mire,
And kings and priests, a strange and mournful list.
O ancient river ! flowing to the sea,
What voices haunt my wildered memory !

Greece

LAND of the sun-born statues! Land of song!
Land of the hero, where the sacred sea
Forever lifts its chant of liberty
Upon thine ancient shores! Our spirits long
To catch the grace and beauty that belong
To thy great teachers; grace and beauty born
In hearts as fresh and native as the morn
That breaks upon thy hills. Thy subtle tongue
Lives yet, and richly flows from myriad lips
Like honey from Hymettus, and, O Greece!
We sail forever for the golden fleece,
And with Achilles leave the tents and ships
To raze great-gated Ilium, and stand
Victorious upon the red-wet strand.

Rome

I

ALMOST four times have seven ages past
Over thy head, great Rome! and still thy heart
Beats strong, and in thy awful mien thou art
Thyself, e'en now, though shorn of all.   How vast
The shadow from thy form majestic cast
Upon the vale of time!   Thy fatal dart
Long kept the world submissive while thy part
Of rulership was finely borne.   Thou hast
Still on thee shadows of thy purple vest;
As when the captive nations swelled thy train
And sadly sang to thee their suppliant strain,
When marvelled at thee all the East and West.
For glory thou didst fill the world with gloom,
And so I hail thy fall, Imperial Rome!

II

THE Pagan world knelt at thy jewelled feet,
Whose gods within thy fanes did consecrate
Her tributary gold: whose sons did wait
Within thy palaces and oft defeat
Thy potent will, and seize thy throne with fleet
And iron arm.   Thy mighty emperors
Sprang chiefly from the barbarian shores

And from the tent strode to thy lofty seat
Of majesty : yet thou didst Latinize
Them all, them and the world, and magnify
Thyself alone.   Thy magic wand did lie
On continent and sea, and solemnize
With name of Roman tribes without a name,
And in remotest regions write thy fame.

III

IT is a pure and lovely company
Of men and women, for the most part slaves,
Greek in their language, who among the graves
And excavated places lift on high
Their patient hearts, while raging death draws nigh
And martyr-crowns.   The holy bishop laves
Unnoted thousands in the tide that saves
Beyond the fiery trial ; tidings fly
In secret of the One whose sacrifice
Sufficeth for the world's uncounted sins,   ＾
And heaven a throng of holy converts wins ;
Who in their dying scatter seeds that rise
In larger harvests still.   And lo ! great Rome
Of Christ's religion is the cherished home.

IV

PRIDE of the saint, and light of many lands
Beyond the utmost bounds of all the West!
For ages thou didst keep the truth confest
Of Peter and of Paul, but as thy hands
Grew strong and riches flowed to thee like sands
Upon the shore, thou couldst no longer rest
In thy simplicity, but with unblest
Desire of earthly splendor made demands
Upon it for thy rites, and made the faith
Of Christ a ceremony burdensome,
Which like a veil obscured the dome
Of spiritual attainment; the path
To heaven was something to be sought
With sordid gold, not with Christ's merit bought.

V

DRUNK with iniquity and blind with pride
Of place and power, thou wouldst not hear the cry
Of nations for true Christian liberty:
Thou wouldst not see the deep and strenuous tide
Of reformation loosening from thy side
Thy offspring of a thousand years; thine eye,
All bleared with sin, saw not the unity

Of ages falling : Thou wert satisfied
To curse thy children and to drink thy fill
Of heathen sweets.   O Papacy ! the foe
Of justice.   What immitigable woe
Shall yet o'ertake thee in the calm and still
Security of noon ! What thunder blast
Shall shiver thee to atoms at the last !

Italy

O ITALY! Fair Italy! The earth
Is full of echoes from thy dreamy past,
And everywhere the shadows dimly vast
Fall from thy form : thou hadst thy wondrous birth
Like Venus from some rosy spray.   Thy hearth
Resounds with song, and on thy walls do last
The mind's heroic images.   Thou hast
A voice in which a thousand strains of worth
Blend in triumphant harmony, which leads
Us captive all, while countless ghosts sublime
March past us from the depths of ancient time,
And memory rings with clang of valiant deeds.
Mother of beauty and immortal gifts !
Would thou hadst Truth which blesses and uplifts.

The Middle Ages

I

THE scene is filled with hierarchs and kings,
With castles and cathedrals dim and vast,
And all the knightly tourneys of the past,
And splendors chivalrous which fancy flings
Bright over all.   Who would not covet wings
With which to track his way through ages gone ?
So he might join some bright procession
Of pilgrims to the holy wells and springs,
Where haloed saints in mossy hermitage
Fasted the lingering years ; or to the hills
Of Palestine, where Salem's vision fills
The heart with dreadful awe.   Mysterious age !
Thee I would visit though I would not stay,
And with thy shadowy dreams beguile a day.

II

GREAT age! though filled with many childish things
Which we have put away.   Thy rightful place
In history is felt by those who trace
In sequence just the world's great course, which brings
Its life through thee.   Thy deathless shadow clings
To all our institutes : in law thy face
Is seen, and in the blood of all our race

69

Thy spirit lives.   To us thy Dante sings.
Thy gentle monks lived not for self alone,
But left their hearts for us in carved stone,
And scrolls illuminate with lines untold
And learned dialectic.   Thy strong towers
Speak to our noblest tastes, and from the cold
Bleak past thou offerest us some fragrant flowers.

III

I COUNT him blind, or one who reads in vain
The world's immortal history, whose soul
Exults not when he hears called out the roll
Of mediæval names, and cannot gain
New inspiration for his will and brain
When well he studies the illumined scroll
Of all their matchless deeds.   Art had its school
With grave philosophy, and without pain
Wrought nothing great in song and sacred shrine :
It told us how religion should indwell
All life and thought, and, with its potent spell,
Involve the nations in a light divine.
The page of beauty by great poets penned
To latest ages then high fame shall send.

IV

THEY had their superstitions and their crimes,
Their feudal bondages and rash crusades,
Their petty tyrants and their ruthless raids ;
They had, but so they had their silver chimes,
Their gentle homes of prayer and holy times
Of festival and song.   In hills and glades,
By winding rivers and 'neath forest shades,
In realms remote and in Cisalpine climes
Was heard the sound of never-ceasing chant,
And praise perpetual.   They have their part
In Time's great chronicle, and on the chart
Of human progress left no mean and scant
Inditing.   Like stained windows they convey
To us the light that fell upon their day.

V

IN your wide furrows were the fruitful seeds
Of whole milleniums of thought and work,
And in your famous monuments there lurk
True lessons for our own deep future needs.
The world before you throbbing with its deeds
Of wondrous glory did not die unheired,
And our great modern centuries are reared

Upon your own stability.   Your weeds
We dry and label and keep safe : your flowers
We plant anew and with them decorate
Our page ; and standing at the open gate
Of coming times we see your minster towers
Still casting peaceful shadows on the earth,
And bearing witness to your faith and worth.

Cathedrals

DEAR images of faith profound : Sweet songs
In stone ; pictures of grace victorious
Over man's shapeless aims ! could he rear thus
His ladders into heaven, while feudal wrongs
Attended superstitious fears, and prongs
Oppressive goaded human life ? when light
Of earthly hope grows dim then shines heaven's
       bright
And beauteous flame ; the soul repines and longs
For unseen succors, upward sends its prayer
And lives for God. Then, all attired in grace
And holiness and trust, it fills the air
With sacred hymns, anoints its glowing face,
And consecrates to Christ its gifts so fair,
And makes its home within the holy place.

The Jordan

O SAD soft river rushing like a tide
Of leaping glories to no living sea !
With awe I ponder thy long history.
Forever with thy name there must abide
A holy spell.   Thy yellow waves that wide
Asunder rolled that Israel might pass
To conquest and a home, seem like a glass
Of that last boundary o'er which we glide
To our immortal joy : and since that Christ
Within thy blissful waters set His feet
Thou art to us all consecrate and sweet,
And murmurest ever of the meek Baptist.
Roll on, roll on, O waves, beneath the sun,
And brighten ever as you glance and run !

Elijah

TREMENDOUS day in Israel's history
When with Elijah heathen prophets stood
On Carmel's slope, and on the piléd wood
Laid sacrificial beasts, perchance to see
If Baal were divine, or at his plea
The God of Israel's prophet might send flood
Of fire to burn the calves, and show who should
Be worshipped in the land! All day they dree
The tedious hours: with knives the heathens gash
Themselves: Elijah mocks their god; when, lo!
From heaven falls vengeful fire, and pagans rash'
Are overwhelmed with wrath and deathly woe.
Our sacrifice we lay with this desire,
Let Him be God that answereth by fire.

David

ARISE, anoint him, this is he ! Lo ! here
The monarch comes, all crowned with health alone,
That had some shaded hillock for a throne
Beneath a canopy of palms. What cheer
Lights up his ruddy looks ! How bright and clear
Those eyes that watched the stars when day was done
Mid silent hills ! What soft yet manful tone
Is in that voice that sang of Israel's fear,
Who led him out of Egypt when a child !
Son of the people is he, young and strong,
Whose foes he shall subdue though thousands filed
Up Jordan's vales. Valiant shall be his song
Upon the harp, yet oft so sweet and mild
That men shall for the heavenly kingdom long !

Ezekiel

THE captives by the river sat all sad
And downcast, hanging up the tuneless harp
As through their spirits went the sudden, sharp
Remembrance of fair Sion's songs, when glad
Resounding trumpets filled the fane.   Then had
Ezekiel, priest and seer, seen heaven ope
Her azure gates, and show the realms of hope,
And visions of God's beauty, which should add
New sweetness to His word.   A river clear
Runs through our earthly soil, in which we trace
The regal glory for our light and cheer:
We see in symbol through the stainless space
And heaven's unutterable depths : So near
The banished gazer shines the Father's face.

Saint Paul

O GREAT Apostle ! The Ambassador
Of heaven and Minister of Jesus Christ
To countless souls ! Doth not in this consist
Thy glory eminent, that thou the door
Of Faith didst ope to Gentiles, such as wore
No shadow of the ancient truth, but dwelt
Outside in deepest gloom, and ne'er had felt
The fascination of the Hebrew lore ?
What great humility was thine to serve
The meanest of mankind, and put away
Thy patriot pride, thy past forget, nor swerve
From boundless labors when thy Strength and Stay
Invisible remained ! I pray for nerve
Like thine to stand out in the evil day.

Saint Columba

THE halo round thy head is formed of mist
Out of the ancient sea, thou glorious saint
Of weird Iona ! on it is no taint
Of city-glare, but it is brightly kist
Of purest sunbeams.   Great Evangelist
Of Celtic lands ! well do I hear the plaint
Of ocean with thy holy chant keep faint
Harmonious antiphon.   Did ye not wist,
O waves, what duteous voice gave utterance
To psalms and hymns and spiritual songs
Amid your solitary bounds ?   It haunts
You yet, and on your onward path prolongs
Its deep reverberations, like the chants
With which the angels soothe our human wrongs.

Baptism of Ethelbert of Kent

THOU happy monarch ! snatched from pagan gods
And with pure waters cleansed from every sin ;
What unknown sun has dawned and smiled within
All Saxon-land ! What joy in the abodes
Of blessed heaven as Austin shods
The King for Christ's bright path, this glorious day !
The King is Christ's, and all that own his sway
Shall hear and turn, and all the merry roads
Be bright with pilgrims to this fountain sweet,
Upsprung in Kentish soil.   God's kingdom here
Comes down, and angels walk with unseen feet
Ways haunted once by horrid sprites of fear
And loathly ill ; and in the pearly street
The King and thousands walk with vision clear.

Venerable Bede

LONG centuries have held in their embrace,
O venerable Bede! thy gentle soul :
But never have they blotted out the scroll
Of thy achievements. Of our Saxon race
Thou wert the best, and sittest in the place
Of highest honor midst its dead. How fair
Thy life, which was a golden psalm, a prayer,
Immortal melody of love! We trace
Thy holy years from childhood up, that trod
At seven the sacred cloister, and grew on
To priesthood and to wisdom, with thy God
Conversing ever like the holy John,
Whose gospel thou translatedst ; then with rod
Of God in hand went forth, thy labor done.

Thomas Cranmer

In learning great, greater in gentleness,
Dear Master of our tongue's rich subtleties!
Thy lot was cast in troublous times, when wise
It was to hide away from fame, confess
No purpose, and awake no fears.   I bless
Thy memory, meek saint! whoever plies
Against it bitter words.   Who willing dies
For truth a martyr is.   In storm and stress
I know thy weakness, but I know thy might.
What endless praise shall cleave to thy last hour,
When with thine erring hand that seemed to blight
Thy past thou didst embrace the fiery shower!
Mercy for all was thy grand litany;
And mercy all might nobly show to thee.

Richard Hooker

WISEST among the sages ! Of the saints
Tenderest and fairest! Like some great star
That hides its brightest beams in heaven afar,
And unawares our darkness sweetly paints
With tranquil light, he kindly shines, nor faints
Ever on earth.   Dear, simple, holy one !
England were great if thou wert all alone
Her theologian.   Thy deep complaints
God only heard.   In utter lowliness
Among the lowly thou didst hide away,
To write for future ages, and to bless
Vast multitudes that own and love thy sway ;
Spirits that never saw thy modest face
Shall hail and kiss thee in eternal day!

Launcelot Andrewes

SAINTLY among the saints, how fair thy fame
Among the brethren of the way of life !
Serene amidst the noisy paths of strife
Thou walkedst freely without breath of blame.
With brow anointed by celestial flame,
Thou failedst not to shine when sin was rife
On every hand : like a glittering knife
Thy learning smote that ancient Papal shame
That still lives on.   But thou didst not ascend
Alas ! the primate-throne, a higher thine
In brighter worlds, where never any friend
Can pass away, nor foe invade, where shine
Saints like thyself, who on their God attend
Unrestingly, and near Him, wax divine.

Joseph Butler

GREAT Master! Spirit calm and clear! To thee
We owe an everlasting recompense,
Who into our stern darkness, drear and dense,
Brought from the awful depth, eternity,
A little shaft of light, and mad'st us see
Our limits and our human impotence.
Beyond the veil thou hast departed hence,
Where 'neath the shade of immortality
Thou walkest with some friend, and in the light
Canst spell the mysteries of Paradise.,
How dost thou feel the vision infinite
Thrill all thy soul! How pure within thine eyes
Must glow prophetic thought when in the height
Thou see'st the workings of the Only Wise!

Jonathan Edwards

THROUGH farthest regions of the light he passed
E'en while he toiled among New England hills.
A spirit open to the sun, which fills
With radiant prophecy, in which is glassed
Heaven's holiest images, was his.   So fast
Upon the rock his feet were set that storms
Of earth he felt not: men he counted worms
Amidst the mire, and looked for feet that haste
On awful judgment hitherbound.   To him
Sin and its doom alike were terrible
And hell more vast than heaven, but what a hymn
Of beauty was his life!   The heart will dwell
Delighted on his faith and zeal sublime
Which on the forests laid their gentle spell.

The Church of England

WHAT dignity and what simplicity
Are thine, dear mother Church! Thy sons of old
Lived in an atmosphere above earth's cold
And misty levels, and thy liturgy,
So strong and pure and of unwisdom free,
Adorns thee like a crown of finest gold.
Thy voice is rich and deep, not harsh nor bold,
But clear, like reverend bells across the lea,
Toned to the note of benediction
And love divine.   Thy heart within is sound,
Thy white-robed squadrons are fast hast'ning on
To bear good tidings to earth's utmost bound.
Already thou dost dwell in every zone;
England through thee is consecrated ground.

Homer

HERO ample-browed, sublime Enchanter
Of the early world ! O Thou good and wise !
Thy signature of greatness broadly lies
On all thy works. For Troy I would not err
With those who make thee but a ghost, a mere
Dim mist of Phantasy. I see thee rise
Like morning when around him all the skies
Put on his livery, for bards most dear
In every clime take on thy light, and bask
Each in his little glade lit up by thee.
Pellucid fountain ! one could never ask
An art more glorious than this—so free
To fall in showers refreshing, as if task
'Twere not to echo far the sounding sea.

Dante

OF all that walked in hell thou, thou alone
Didst cast a shadow on the lurid cloud,
Immortal Bard !   Alone among the crowd
That daily vexed thee here thou seem'st to own
Unfading influence.   That heart is stone
That melts not when thy voice all clear and loud
Amidst th' abyss of flame is smit with proud
Emotion masterful, or tender tone
Takes on among the ardent happy throng
That rests within the golden gleaming mist,
And lifts aloft its pure, ecstatic song.
Thine exile ended, thou art keeping tryst
With radiant guide, and ancient poet strong,
And dwelling in whatever light they list.

Geoffrey Chaucer

APOLLO·LIKE, and young, thou art a Greek
Almost, yet Saxon in thy love of tint,
And Norman in thy tastes.   Life without stint
Is in the scenes set forth by thee : no weak
Nor wooden pilgrims pass us by to seek
For sin's indulgence in great Canterbure.
Nature o'ercomes thy art, which cannot cure
Nor change the homely herd.   We hear them speak
To us through all the Mediæval years
And centuries since, and 'tis no solemn tongue,
Such as was spoken by the Hebrew seers,
But light and joyous, springlike, as a song
Of birds among the blossoms : with pure tears
It does not tremble, nor with dread of wrong.

John Milton

Ah! human angel! wanderer through realms
Which only wingéd feet will dare to tread,
Whose spirit with the gracious dawn is wed,
The torrent of thy song quite overwhelms
Earth-hindered man.   Thou saw'st the pluméd helms
Of God's immortal sons, when onward led
Against His foes, and gazed, while chaos fled :
So clear had been thine eye as human films
Had by the great Archangel been removed.
With love thou buildedst in the lofty rhyme,
And all the treasures of our language proved ;
Brought shadows of eternity o'er time,
And made thy solemn measures to be loved
By all whose steadfast spirit is sublime !

George Herbert

DEAR soul, that early trod the unseen way,
Yet gave us songs and precepts for our age !
Blest is our lot and great our heritage,
Who know and love thy voice !   Thy Sunday lay
Comes home to weary hearts that every day
With sin and want unfailing warfare wage ;
Our gloom is broken by thy shining page,
Where precious thoughts, like gems, with sunbeams
     play.
The temple by thy gifts is glorified,
The priest is brighter since thou wert so bright ;
Religion points to thee with joy and pride,
As one shot through and through with heavenly light,
Who all her purest teachings justified,
And made her sweet and precious in men's sight.

Thomas Ken

O HEART of strength and wondrous tenderness,
Jewelled and dazzling with all gifts of light,
Pure as the dawn upon an Alpine height,
Receive the homage of the sons of grace!
What mystic love upon thy brow may trace
Of bliss and sweetness, in the regions bright
Where of the throne itself thou catchest sight,
I cannot tell; but blessed is the place
Where thou dost walk! There angels congregate
To sing with thee dear hymns to God on high:
There seraphs clothed with ardent flame still wait
Upon thy gracious soul, and turn love's sigh
To golden mist, that may adorn the gate
When morn and eve the great King passes by.

Samuel Taylor Coleridge

WHAT singer of them all, great melodist!
Had sweetness quite like thine! Deep interfused
With all thy thought, as if thou oft hadst mused
In Paradise, or dwelt in dreamy mist
Of mountains twilight-purpled, or hadst kissed
The tears from Spenser's face, is wondrous balm
Which overflows thy thought, and through the calm
Rich texture of thy cadence lives. Like list
Of hero-names in Homer or the names
Of lands and cities in my Milton flow
Thy numbers marvelous. Among the fames
Most glorious is thine. While tempests blow
Upon the sea, and roar the rhythmic flames,
And rivers run to song, that fame shall glow.

William Wordsworth

LET me invoke thy presence, Heart of gold !
For sure thou ling'rest where the hills stretch blue
And far. Sure in these waters must the true
Reflection of thy face be seen : these old
And solemn forests must thy spirit hold,
At least when rare deep sunset brings the dew,
And to its fading all the stars ensue !
What mystic glory did thy birth enfold !
What genius led thee out each morning fair
To turn the waters into thoughts, and touch
The rocks with spiritual grace, and care
For truth that sings within the cowslip !   Much
We owe to thee, for thou hast everywhere
Seen visions of calm joy, and given us such.

Alfred Tennyson

AND is it true that radiant richness dwells
In Saxon speech, and perfect thoughts can match
With perfect forms ? What gleamings didst thou catch
From passing unseen wings, whose great verse tells
Of beauty paramount, and gently swells
With pulses of the heart ?   O ! thou didst watch
Where others only passed, and didst unlatch
The unaccustomed doors, and of deep wells
In woods untrodden took'st thy fill.   Awake
Thou wert to inner charms of song, and felt
A motion from the world's deep soul, that brake
O'er thee in thrills mysterious.   Hearts melt
With thine ; and at thy sculptured fountain slake
Their thirst, whose longings thou hast known and spelt.

John Keble

BEAUTEOUS spirit! Sweet and primitive,
Bard of the soul! That walked in Godly fear
Through all the cycle of the Christian year,
And taught us how the child of light should live
Among these earthly shadows fugitive :
Well didst Thou interweave the Autumn sere
With childhood's innocence and hearty cheer.
Thou gavest all thy gentle heart could give
To gentle hearts.   Thou didst with grace unfold
In flowers and sunbeams and in hills and vales
Pictures of heavenly beauty.   Lights untold
Lie open in thy gracious hymn when pales
Our daily sun, and in the realms of gold
Such words shall breath when earthly being fails.

Arthur Cleveland Coxe

FATHER in God! most reverend and bright!
True Singer in this vineyard of the West!
That shed a tender gleam upon the breast
Of earth, and bathed the village spire in light
Of filial love; that walked so long in white
Among us here; now on the sunlit crest
Of some high hill thou sittest with the blest,
And singest lyric notes with all thy might
Which echo to the throne.   We cannot weep
For thee, for thou hast gained thy deep repose,
And near the altar-shade wilt vigil keep
With them that like thee wait till Sion's woes
Are past, and all the saints that fell on sleep
Awake, and sing, and blossom as the rose.

A Many Pinnacled

A MANY pinnacled upon the fame
Of ancestry hold fairly well their place;
But oh! how many without wit or grace
Shame both the past and present! They who came
To these our Western shores, men without blame,
Men unimpeached and unimpeachable,
With iron wills and with no souls to sell
For earthly price, should have for sons the same
Great-moulded sort of men as they themselves.
Americans! Fear the degenerate days
When to be Pagan is to win all praise
From multitudes that put away on shelves
Their bibles, and on Sundays shun the church,
And leave our pure Religion in the lurch.

God's Tabernacle

O LORD my God! this earth Thy palace is:
In gladness and in love Thou didst create
Its lofty frame and clothe it with so great
And various beauty.   In the abyss
Of light, amidst innumerous worlds this
One receives Thy special care.   Thou dost wait
That Thou may'st gracious be to man whose state
So wretched is through sin; yea! from Thy bliss
Descendest here, and dwellest with Thine own,
And diest for them, suffering all pain.
O may Thy mercies not be all in vain!
May millions penitent before Thy throne
Pour out their hearts! and do Thou walk with us,
And truth unfold in visions glorious.

Christ in Us

CHRIST in us the hope of glory is, so
I believe, and seek for Him within me.
He that came to earth doth come to free
Each soul that will receive Him from the slow,
Sad death of sin. 'Tis He who changes woe
And weakness into joy and strength, and wakes
Us from our sloth to hear the song that makes
The heavens rejoice, proclaiming love. The glow
Of trusting faith in God is interfused
With all my thoughts; submission is the crown
He wreathes my brow withal, on which flows down
The fragrant oil of kingly might. Accused
Of evil I can claim His pardoning grace;
Dejected, I can look to His bright face.

Is There no Costly Ointment?

Is there no costly ointment I can find
To shed upon my dear Redeemer's feet
While here He sits so gentle and so sweet,
And folds us in His smile and eyes most kind?
What can He care for gold or gems consigned
With state upon His altar, when men fleet
So swiftly from it to the joys unmeet
Of witless luxury? What swelling wind
Of melody can reach His heart, what hymn,
In which the joy and wondrous mystery
Of human love for God breathes not its sigh
Brought from a spirit welling to the brim?
O Jesus! let me love Thee with my soul,
Then shall I find some offering to unroll.

What Myriad Rivers

WHAT myriad rivers, thou insatiate sea,
Dost thou imbibe through ages dim and hoar !
Whose silvery music mingles evermore
With thy all-conquering song.   Eternally
They softly gleam and glide and run to thee,
Yet never do they fail.   Like wise men's lore
They thrive by giving, and so freely pour
Their generous waves through many a grassy lea,
And bank elm-shadowed into thy vast breast ;
And ne'er abate their melody by night
Or day, nor sparkle with a shade less bright,
But in their flowing deem that they are blest.
My child, this needful lesson duly learn—
They keep their life who serve another's turn.

Ember Day

ALL day I labor in His vineyard here,
    And often pray and think about what next
    Should be performed of duty, or what text
Of Holy Writ will best unfold some clear
And edifying thought for those whom fear
    Doth hinder, or who often are perplext
    With doubt and conflict. And, oh! Thou that deck'st
These hills with ripening fruits, I often hear
    The voice which said: "The laborers are few."
And then I hear the perilous sounds without
Of them that for Thy vine's destruction shout;
    And feel how weak I am to face this crew.
Do Thou, to make me zealous in the strife,
Mix heavenly spices with the wine of life.

How Blest Are They that By all Waters Sow

How blest are they that by all waters sow
Immortal seed! Ours is a task sublime,
Who lead men up beyond the vale of time
To where the mountains of attainment glow
With spiritual lustre.   Here below
We pass for spies, who have been through that clime
And learned a little of its saintly rhyme
To charm men's hearts, and from a fragment
    show
How wonderful our Father's country is.
Inopportune is never any hour
Wherein to gladden with His promises
Sin-wearied souls, and show the gracious power
Of their most dear Redeemer.   O what bliss
When opens in them Faith's unfading flower!

The Gifts of God

GOD'S gifts are perfect, in their motive pure,
Pure as the sunbeams in the heart of flowers,
And constant in their flow as are the hours
That still glide on.   Like Him they shall endure,
And all our sorrows and our trials cure,
Increasing in their value till the towers
Of venture highest, holiest, are ours
Far in the land of light.   Us they allure
Into the wilderness to walk with God:
And on through strife and labor to the stream
That borders on the gardens where the road
Leads to the golden city.   Ye misdeem
That falter on beneath your heavy load,
And will not slake your darkness with His beam.

The Alchemist

A STRANGE pathetic picture like a dream
Of dissapointed hope that hopes again,
Lives in the ages past all clear and plain,
The Alchemist into the fiery stream
That carries off his wealth throws all the cream
Of brain and energy, looking in his pain
For gold from metals base : sometimes in vain
Imagining he sees the precious gleam.
Yet is the picture not all sad : he finds
Not what he seeks, but by an accident
Nature gives up some secret, as from blent
Rich fluids issue wonderful unwinds.
In life's ambitions fail we often may,
But, God be praised ! good do we by the way.

O Let This Be My Portion with the Blest!

O LET this be my portion with the blest,
 To see Him risen up to shut the door,
 To hear him gently say, for evermore ;
To look, to love, to lean upon His breast,
To hear the pulses of His soul confest
 While slowly He unfolds the precious store,
 Which all the years for me he gladly bore,
Of love unspeakable ; to look and rest,
 And feel His tears in silence once again
Shed over me as whilom from His cross,
 When love and pity mingled with His pain,
He counted earth and heaven and all but loss
 That me, even me, He might forever gain
To be through Him made clean from earthly dross !

Our Feet Shall Stand within Thy Gates

OUR feet shall stand within thy gates, O dear
Jerusalem !   Here do we travel on
Hardly bestead till days long hours be gone,
And wonder when we shall behold with clear
Untroubled eyes Thy lofty towers, and near
Thee draw with songs and everlasting joy
Upon our heads.   What hopes do we employ
Our moments with, when worn with toil or fear,
We seek some shelter in the wilderness,
Where we may sit, and weave upon the air
Some picture out of sunshine, sweet and fair,
And call it by Thy name ; and often bless
Thy open gates and glories faintly seen—
Unshadowed deeps of gold and purple sheen !

The Psalms

A PALACE rises in its calm repose
Before me in the wilderness, as fair
As morning when upon the tender air
She rears her dome in color like a rose.
Within a calm melodious music flows,
In which impleached are gleams of gold, and rare
Pale lights of silvery hue.   'Tis like a prayer
Of saint that was a sinner, in which glows
The vivid shaft of light mid subtle glooms.
The windows brighten with each radiant morn,
And with the evening pale to softest blooms
Of ruddy glory, printing on forlorn
Repentant souls sweet images of dooms
Prepared for victors in the world new-born.

Te Deum Laudamus

EXALTED strain!   The Church's jubile hymn
And creed and supplication all in one,
Touched with a penitential tone since won
One rest is not: a window in our dim
And narrow life, where heavenly light doth limn
A mystic vision in the hues of earth.
We more and more discern its priceless worth,
And fill the cup of music to the brim
To give it overflow.   The melody
Of voices from the saintly past I hear,
Like murmurs of the shining summer sea,
Bringing the Church's solemn memories near,
As if from islands in eternity—
Voices of victory, awful and dear.

The Collects

ADOWN the long nave of the Christian year
Those saintly windows oft by hands unknown
Wrought for us, in the ages past, alone
Surpass all mortal worth.   How justly dear
The meaning in their limnéd forms which wear
The light of heavenly truth! Christ on His throne
And on His cross, in Salem with His own,
In lilied fields and on the crystal mere
Is their great theme, while a vast multitude
In sanctity pre-eminent, and crowned
With grace are there, and all the blissful brood
Of angels bright.   There Charities are found
In white arrayed or golden robed, and food
For Faith to feed on till the trumpet sound.

Brought to Baptism

HERE have ye brought this child to be baptized,
Ye faithful ones!   God shall reward your care,
And this sweet babe shall henceforth duly share
The heritage of saints.   Oh! who hath prized
So great a gift enough, or hath surmised
The greatness of the love that now to prayer
And faith descends to make us clean and fair,
So angels may attend us, lest, advised
Of evil, we submit, and win not heaven.
Dear little one!   Thou shall be gently fed
With sacred food free from all earthly leaven :
The Shepherd Good that all thy fathers led
Shall lead thee too, and when the shadowy even
Surrounds thy soul, He shall lift up thine head.

Public Catechising

IT is a sight that gladdens and inspires
When parish children meet at evensong
Within the holy place, and hear the strong
Deep burden of the word, and feel the fires
Of ages burn upon their hearts: in choirs
They sing their tender hymns, and then await
The pastor's questions, near the chancel gate
All duly ranged, as long ago their sires,
In whose strong faith they walk. Doctrine and duty,
Sacrament and prayer, and the holy vows
Made at the font, when on their infant brows
The cross was signed, in fresh sweet light they see.
O Pastors! be ye diligent and wise,
And in your solemn churches catechize.

Voices of Children

O little melodies that fill the air
Like wingéd joys arrayed in silver beams,
You make the world a realm of gentle dreams,
And spread before me visions sweet and fair!
Your voices, dearest children, in which care
Has made no rift, flow on like limpid streams
O'er rosy rocks, and blend in gleeful screams
In one cascade of sound! Would I were there
To drown my heart in your dear tender mirth,
And be a child again a little while!
What grace is Childhood's, innocent and free,
Pure as the freshest dawn, and without guile!
Thou hast a beautiful eternity,
O child! Thy mother-world shall thrill and smile
For ever, when she hears, and thinks on thee.

The Sacrifice

"GOD will provide Himself a lamb, my son!"
So Abraham to Isaac, and they two
Went on.   They climbed the hill beneath the blue
Bright morn, silent as death, as if to stone
And adamant the world had turned, and moan
Must not be heard on that highway.   " How few
His years and fair ! " bethought the sire so true
And kind," yet let God's sovereign will be done !"
The soft winds played about the boy's bright locks
And sunbeams on his brow their blessings laid ;
O agony ! O faith ! O silent rocks !
O heart that naught can ever make afraid !
And God received the lamb for sacrifice,
And gave it back to faithful heart and eyes.

Elisha's Bones

It was a happy chance, as men would say,
That gave revival to a burnt-out life ;
When frightened sore by Moab's band of strife
They waited not their dead to put away
In grave for it prepared, but turned to lay
It in Elisha's tomb.   Lo ! How their grief
Fled far with Death surprised ; whose thraldom brief
At touch of saintly bones was like the play
Of lightning, that startles and is gone.   So
Let darker shadows intercept our gloom,
And from unnoted founts fresh comfort flow.
We sadly think we have caught up with doom
Only to find our hearts with rapture glow,
When withered hopes revive in Jesus' tomb !

O When Shall All This World

OH ! When shall all this world that Thou hast made
Acknowledge Thee, Great King! When shall the
    lands
That lie in darkness stretch their open hands
To Thee for light, and on Thy gracious aid
Lean willingly ! When shall the awful shade
Of death pass from our race, and we take on
Our destined sanctity ! Oh ! from Thy throne
Look down, and to all Christian men afraid
To give themselves and all they have to Thee,
Give strength Divine, that so Thy will supreme
May lead them on to drive the heathen dream
From this Thy world ! We never shall be free
To bring all men to Thee, till we bring all
We are and have and love when Thou dost call !

With Him in the Holy Mount

OH! May we not with Jesus make our way
To where the cloud rests on the mountain top,
As if the open heavens of God will drop
Down righteousness, and there behold Him pray,
And manifest His glory? May we stay
While saints adore their King, and of His death
And passion speak: and feel the soothing breath
Of heaven about our brows? Shall inner day
Unfold upon the night its sevenfold beam
And bathe us in its tender waves of gold,
That through eternal years have calmly rolled
From sphere to sphere? Shall we forget our dream
Of sorrow for a while, and talk of joy?
Our hours with Him we thus may oft employ.

Lest Ye be Faint

LEST ye be faint and weary in your minds,
Consider Him, O Christians ! that endured
The scornful words of sinful men. Allured
Are all our hearts by Him who binds
Our safety with His life, and round us winds
His cords of love. These hearts shall be assured
Before Him Who through sacrifice has cured
Them of the primal fault, and always finds
In pity how His pardon He shall show,
When oft we grieve Him kind. Ah ! Blessed One !
Thou diedst, but our spirits gently flow
Along the even beds of peace, and shun
The peril and the pain. We cannot know
How much Thou spentest for our kingdom won !

Joy

WHO that has joy hears not some undertone
Of sadness stealing through the usual theme
Of His continual song, and will not deem
His life monotonous if joy alone
His portion were ! 'Twould be a heavy stone
To weigh him down, and make this living seem
A kind of folly, and a mordant dream.
Joy is itself when underneath its throne
Sorrow is chained, not lost to memory,
So he may see from what a bitter woe
And servitude he has been freed. Thus he
Rejoices in his joy, and in its glow
Glories aright—so his humility,
Kept fresh by thought of sorrow, quells the foe.

Paradise

I STAND upon thy threshold and look in,
O Paradise ! Mine eyes droop as in sleep,
While in thy soft and mellow haze they steep
Themselves.   O blissful meadows where no sin
Blights the immortal blooms, where spirits win
With toilless ease essential joys and reap
Unutterable peace ! Who would not keep
Thy sabbaths, all forgetful of the din
Of time's great billows ?   O, thou happy vale !
What music fills my soul with blessedness
Too deep for earth, which memory will fail
To echo when the vision fades !   O, bless
My ears again !   Come quickly like a sail
O'er Summer waves, with messages of peace.

In That Day

WHEN heavens renewed reflect the earth renewed,
And righteousness within them all shall shine
All perfected forever ; there shall swell
Upon the wildered air the song bedewed
Of holiest grace, from that great multitude
Innumerable by man.   Who can tell
Its burden while within this narrow fell
He lingers waiting till the tempest rude
Is past ! O blessed be the certain day
That must o'ertop the hills in God's own time,
When darkness flees away, and light sublime
And unsubduable pours forth its ray
On all created things ! and all respond
As waters to the skies in sunbeams blond !

The Peace of God

'TIS afternoon.   The far-off summer hill
Sleeps in this Sunday glory like a saint
Awaiting resurrection.   Shadows faint
Mysteriously o'er it fall; the still
Sweet gentle fields in slumbrous softness fill
With calm delight the pensive eye.   Complaint
Of beast or bird is not.   Every taint
Of busy life seems banished hence until
The earth seems changed to heaven.   The tender air
Is mildly fragrant with the balm of flowers.
Far off the shining river glides as fair
As glides this mellow flow of quiet hours.
Lo! at his door the pastor, free from care,
Sees stretching far away the heavenly bowers.

Peace is a Pearl

PEACE is a pearl found in the glassy sea
And worn upon the brow of such as dwell
In that far happy land ineffable,
That's hidden in its own deep mystery.
They borrow it who by these angels three
Are visited—Repentance, Faith and Love ;
But here it shines not as it doth above,
But hath a wavering gleam, its purity
Dependeth on the strength of holy light
In which they live and pray, just as a coal
Ripens with flame or pales beneath the flight
Of airy wings ; but oh ! the sacred soul
Shall have it for its own 'mid spirits bright,
And it shall shine like stars about the pole.

The Faithful Pastor

FAR in my heart I have a solemn shrine
    All consecrated to a pastor dear—
True man of God, of love almost divine,
    Whose memory is ever bright and clear.

Oft doth his image stand before my eyes;
    He seems to speak, as in the days of yore,
Some precept holy or some counsel wise,
    Some gentle lesson from his well-wrought store.

Oft in the quiet of his own abode
    From classic pages he would turn away
To talk awhile about the heavenly road,
    And point me to the glad eternal day.

With studies would he mingle holy fires,
    And speak with tongues not used in Greece or
      Rome;
And walking midst the flowers, his pure desires
    Still would be kindling for our Father's home.

In Church he seemed a saintly angel blest,
    A rare beatitude his presence shed;
He lent a beauty to the sacred vest,
    And from our hearts all earthly feeling fled.

The sermon deeply touched the quivering soul,
    And wrought a sense of sin within the breast:
Then Jesus' mercies he would all unroll,
    Forgiveness, victory and endless rest.

Then rare and wonderful it was to see
    With what devout and tender awe he stood
To break the pledge of immortality,
    And give into our hands the heavenly food.

And when he came to bless us all at last,
    We scarce could see his form through blissful
      tears;
Glories and gifts came raining down so fast,
    And love that fills the heart and casts out fears.

Once there was dread and sorrow nigh at hand,
    My sire lay half within the shadowy vale;
The good man came, and all about that land,
    Which Christ prepares he talked till twilight
      pale.

He read the fourteenth chapter of Saint John,
    As only he could read who felt it all:
Then prayed that as in heaven God's glory shone,
    So here on earth His tender light might fall.

They both long since have faded from our view,
　　No more on earth I'll see their kindly forms;
But in the angels' eyes they brighter grew
　　As rainbows brighten after earthly storms.

My God ! I thank Thee that in early years
　　I often saw Thy faithful servant's face,
And that so often now it still appears
　　In vivid vision and with all its grace.

I still would follow where he led the way,
　　And in his shining footsteps place my feet :
I would be worthy, Lord, to dwell alway
　　Where still might be diffused such influence
　　sweet.

I would all pastors might be fashioned so,
　　That strength and healing on their lives might
　　wait :
That all the people might in goodness grow
　　And come with singing unto Sion's gate.

Here then I'll write for all our pastors dear
　　His epitaph, that they may learn it well :
And beg them all to follow very near
　　This pattern true, of whom I joy to tell.

Epitaph.   S. B. B.

To others gentle, to himself severe,
　　Within his face the light of goodness shined ;
Temperate and modest, simple and sincere,
　　His was a chastened soul to God resigned.

One only thought within his bosom reigned—
　　To make Christ precious in the eyes of men :
And now this blest reward he has attained,
　　To rest in peace till Christ shall come again.

The Temporal and the Eternal

How subtle and how fugitive
    Our loftiest thoughts and feelings are!
Some sordid care a moment takes,
    And when we seek they are not there.

So vanish all the fairest things
    That earth or sky can entertain ;
The dewdrop and the sunset glow
    Seem almost to be fair in vain.

Those shadowy lights that sometimes come
    Across our waking, shapes serene
That for majestic moments glide
    Before us in a mystic sheen,

Those wavering pinnacles and domes
    Of thought and prayer that lift the soul,
And tender mists and rosy dreams
    Once touched, away together roll.

It will not be forever thus,
　　The world we seek is brighter far
Than all that's lovely round us here—
　　Sublimer than the mountains are.

Our troubled vision shall grow calm,
　　Like waters when the breezes fail ;
And things too holy to wait long
　　Upon it here, shall never pale.

Thy tranquil eye shall see the king
　　In all His beauty ; then be sure
All else that's holy, fair, divine,
　　Thine eye shall see in regions pure.

The Troubles of this Life

LIFE's troubles in great part are like
    A breath upon the window-pane,
A moment spread across our view,
    And in a moment gone again.

But some are like the nightly frost
    That gathers on the window-pane,
And will not pass until the sun
    Or fire shines out all bright again.

But all shall surely pass away
    That linger on life's window-pane;
We shall look out and see all clear
    When our true Sun shall rise again.

Clear Shining after Rain

OH ! it is sweet to hear the birds
    Sing gaily after lengthened rains,
As if the pent-up melodies
    Mixed with their pleasure subtle pains.

And blessed will it be, my child !
    To let our hearts pour out their songs,
Which grow in us through earthly storms,
    When open heaven to us belongs.

Clear shining after rain, clear notes
    That fill the sky with mystery,
Clear hearts washed free from every sin,
    Clear souls to love, clear eyes to see :

All shall be ours ; the atmosphere
    Of peace and pardon, light and grace
Around us evermore shall fall ;
    For we shall see our Father's face.

To Comfort All that Mourn

MOURNEST thou, friend of the Bridegroom?
    Alas! how dim and poor thine eyes
That see not in this very room
    A glory fairer than the skies.

Jesus is with thee, crowned with light,
    And robed in majesty divine;
The board is spread before thy sight,
    He turns the water into wine.

Be ready always to sit down,
    For His is a perpetual feast;
Each day His love afresh is shown,
    He is the Everlasting Priest.

All days are holy where He is,
    All places clean where He abides;
The air is radiant with bliss,
    Wherein His saving presence hides.

While here with Him I feast and sing,
    The years shall pass away like flowers;
Then like a bird upon the wing
    I'll fly with Him from wintry bowers

To where the light is always calm,
    And mellow breezes fragrant fall,
In time and tune with that pure psalm
    That hallows there the heart of all.

Stir Up Thy Strength and Come and Help Us

O LET Thy cross give forth new light
    Through all the nations far and wide ;
Dawn on man's bleared and blinking sight,
    O vision of the Crucified !

Stir up in us the will to grow
    From weakness unto living strength ;
Cause us the way of life to know,
    That we may reach the goal at length.

Convert our power to power like thine,
    And our poor love make love indeed :
That we may work Thy work divine
    And help to fill the human need.

The world lies unconverted yet,
    Because we are unworthy Thou
Shouldst bring the nations to forget
    The idols under which they bow.

If we would trample on our sin
    The world would raze its heathen fanes,
Then Thou wouldst wholly enter in
    And consecrate our streets and lanes.

In clothing soft Thy prophets walk,
    And dwell in royal courts at ease,
And spirits perish while they talk
    Of only what their patrons please.

Raise up Thy power and come anear
    And quicken us to do Thy will—
That will so holy and austere—
    Renew it in us ever still.

Make us to dread Thy vengeance now
    Lest when too late we turn to see
The recompense for broken vow—
    A shattered immortality!

Our Shield and Our Reward

WAITING for Thy salvation, Lord,
  I pass the days and years,
Through famine, exile, suffering
  I see Thy hand appears.

'Tis Thou that leadest us along
  Like sheep from hill to vale,
And feedest us with daily bread,
  E'en when our pastures fail.

Sad and forsaken in the land
  We find Thee strong and true—
A friend that never left alone
  The hearts that near Thee drew.

Our pilgrimage is nearly o'er—
  The few and evil days—
Our home stands out before our eyes,
  The realm of endless praise.

From death to life we quickly pass,
  From darkness into light :
And angels carry up our souls
  To walk with Thee in white !

The Father Seeketh Worshippers

THE Father seeketh worshippers
 Among the sons of time,
That in His angels' melodies
 May take their part sublime.

I marvel when I read the words,
 " The Father seeketh such,"
What love is this that stoops to earth
 Our laggard souls to touch

With spirit and with truth divine,
 With fire and vision clear,
That we may rightly worship Him,
 And at His throne appear !

Long have we spent our sighs in vain,
 With earthliness oppressed :
For things that perish in the use
 Forgot what's first and best ;

But heed me now this gracious word,
    "The Father seekest you,"
And be henceforth His worshippers,
    And sing his truth anew

With souls that answer to the truth,
    And walk within the light;
Come thou, and sing within us all,
    O Spirit Infinite!

" Would that all the Lord's People were Prophets "

O SLOW of heart that will not take
    God's word and prove it true
By work and love, and for His sake
    Make it of heaven the clue.

Raise up, O Lord, Thy power of old
    And touch the people's heart:
Give them true light and make them bold
    To speak in street and mart.

Raise up Thy witnesses like John,
    That in the ancient flood
Repenting tribes baptized, and won
    Vast multitudes to God.

Be Ruler midst Thine enemies,
    Unloose Thy conquering bands;
For Thou art great and true and wise,
    That all the heaven commands.

The Pastor's Prayer

MAKE me a lamp, and fill me with Thy light,
That through the dark and stormy paths of night
I may lead on some wandering souls to where
The morning soon must break all clear and fair.

Give me the power to do some certain good,
Although it be not all Thy servant would;
Not only when I work and speak and pray,
But even when I rest by night or day.

The rose, unconscious of its fragrance sweet,
Gives pleasure though it have no hands nor feet;
True lives do good when labor turns to rest,
And they who simply look on them are blest.

The rain does good not only when it falls
Upon the famished fields, but after calls
For many days a blessing down from heaven,
From morn till noon, from noon to peaceful even.

So truly, fully would I do each deed
That this should be its lasting, glorious meed,
That never should its benefit be spent
So long as any live for whom 'tis meant.

Shine Thou through all my dim, sequestered hours,
As when I labor with unfolded powers ;
Live Thou through me in others far and near,
To whom at any time I taught Thy fear.

Bless all that ever heard my voice in prayer,
Who lingered when through all the solemn air
Ascended words of living sacrifice,
And grace poured down in torrents from the skies.

Bless all that were regenerate through me,
And knelt within the shadow of the tree;
And all that ever came within the gate—
The needy, weak and sick, and desolate.

I know not what shall be in future years,
I shall not suffer any foolish fears ;
But make me ready for to stay or go
As Thou shalt choose for me, Lord ! be it so.

" He Wist not That it was True "

PETER—the worn Apostle—slept
 Upon his prison bed,
While many in the city wept
 Lest he should join the dead.

But lo ! an angel at his side
 Took off his weary chain,
The iron gate was opened wide,
 And he was free again.

At first he wist not it was true,
 But thought a vision rose
Upon his troubled soul, and drew
 Between him and his woes.

But in the breezes of the night
 His spirit wakened clear,
He knew that now an angel bright
 Had been so very near.

O ! that we all had eyes to see
 Our kind Deliverer
Come to our prison tenderly
 And loose our fetters there !

And think not it must be a dream
    Because so wonderful ;
For nothing can He ever deem
    Too great to save a soul.

Tis not a vision that I see,
    'Tis God Who worketh all—
My God that from eternity
    Comes to my prison wall.

O ! it is true as heaven above,
    His angel I behold,
And He shall bring me in His love
    Within the gates of gold.

God is Greater Than Our Heart

WHEN we choose the evil way,
Fearless of the judgment day,
And from holiness depart,
God is greater than our heart.

When the darkness fills our eyes,
So we see not in the skies
Visions richer than man's art,
God is greater than our heart.

If the light within us burn
Dimly, so we cannot learn
Truths not spoken in the mart,
God is greater than our heart.

Though we take not up the cross
Daily to our worldly loss,
Suffering its healing smart,
God is greater than our heart.

If His finger gently touch
And our heart condemn us much,
Or He smite with heavy dart,
God is greater than our heart.

When we wade through perils deep
And great bitter tears we weep,
Only this can peace impart,
God is greater than our heart.

Then will I most humbly pray
For His mercy in that day:
And with this His word depart,
God is greater than our heart.

For Thou Art with Me

ALTHOUGH my sorrows have been great and sore,
        I will not weep :
The sea of God's sweet mercy I explore
        And find it deep :
The pearl of peace I find for my sad soul ;
And now I know I shall be well and whole.

His care is always tender and so true,
        I will not fear :
His kindness with my trouble always grew
        To soothe and cheer :
His blessing with me doth He always share,
And lo ! He never shutteth out my prayer.

His throne of love stands open to mine eyes ;
        I will not fail
Nor be discouraged since the sacred skies
        Their lights unveil ;
I will go on to learn His gracious will
And He will bear with all my weakness still.

All Day Long the Stars are Shining

ALL day long the stars are shining,
    Though their forms we cannot see :
Their pure glories intertwining
    Make a white immensity.

Seems your life so weak and narrow,
    Children of this mortal day ?
Are you better than the sparrow
    Flitting in the morning ray ?

Ah ! Your influence who can measure ?
    Which unseen is ever felt ;
Like the stars, you have a treasure,
    Which in other lives must melt.

Could those stars undo their being
    When the sunlight hides their beams,
Earth and sun and orbs were fleeing
    Swiftly down destruction's streams.

Influence must work on for ever,
    Even when withdrawn from sight
That which makes it, like a river,
    Flows through regions infinite.

All night long the sun is gleaming
    Over lands unlike our own;
Millions wake while we are dreaming,
    Quickened at his awful throne.

God is working while we're sleeping;
    In His love our spirits share;
And from hill to hill is leaping
    Grace and Providential care.

All the universe is thrilling
    With creative life and power;
Mind-abysses fast are filling
    With an everlasting dower.

We must hope to see but little
    Of the boundless work of love,
Though not e'en a jot or tittle
    Fail its victory to prove.

'Tis enough that God the Holy
    Teaches us to do His will;
And that in a spirit lowly
    We believe and labor still.

One Thing Have I Desired

ONE thing of God I do desire,
    And for it always pray,
That where he lights His sacred fire
    I may forever stay.

Each morn the streams of heavenly grace
    I wish to see flow down:
Each eve I fain would see His face,
    His sceptre and His crown.

Each day I wish to hear the bells
    Upon His priestly dress,
And listen while the trumpet tells
    Of all His righteousness.

Each day I wish to bring my gift,
    And on the altar lay:
And all my wakened powers uplift
    While there I meekly pray.

I wish to sit at Jesus' feet
    While He unfolds the love,
So true and wonderful and sweet,
    That purchased heaven above.

I wish to grow each day like Him,
    Who died upon the tree,
And soon exchange these regions dim
    For bright eternity.

The morning hastens to appear
    When He shall take me home,
O let me bid farewell to fear
    And say, Lord Jesus, come !

The Eucharistic Hour

THE victory is Thine, O Christ!
  The cross set forth Thy power;
And lo! The blessed Eucharist
  Proclaims it at this hour.

In faith we find Thee, Son of God;
  We know Thee, who Thou art!
We come to Thee; and in Thy blood
  Seek peace for every heart.

Over our souls the Spirit broods,
  How calm it is around!
No voice of earthly care intrudes,
  We kneel on holy ground.

Now hear we from the awful throne
  Set in the realms of bliss,
"Lo! This is My Beloved Son,
  In whom My pleasure is."

Our sorrow turns to joy ; our ears
    Are thrilled with solemn strains
Which echo from immortal spheres,
    Where love forever reigns.

O rapture !   When believing souls
    Find Jesus strong and kind,
O'er them from heaven a glory rolls,
    In them the light hath shined.

Awake and Sing

DEAR little souls! awake and sing,
    For this is Christmas Day ;
Angels have long been on the wing
    To light your Saviour's way :
The heavens above are bright and blue,
To God your tender praise is due ;
        Awake and sing,
        Jesus is King,
All on this Christmas Day.

My little lambs, I am so glad
    That Jesus Christ is born,
This world would be so very sad
    Without its Christmas morn ;
But now He brings us all good cheer
And makes us happy every year ;
        Awake and sing ,
        Jesus is King,
All on this Christmas Day.

Our Heavenly Father is so good
    And always kind, I know :
He gives us all our daily food,
    Because He loves us so ;
But now He sends His only Son
To comfort every little one ;
      Awake and sing,
      Jesus is King,
All on this Christmas Day.

I wonder how we all can show
    Our thankfulness and love !
O yes ! we all can daily grow
    Like Him who reigns above :
We all can be more sweet and kind,
Some holy duty we can find ;
      Awake and sing,
      Jesus is King,
All on this Christmas Day.

I love to hear the Christmas bells
    Ring out their merry chime,
It seems as if an angel tells
    The tidings of the time :
It seems as if my heart goes forth
To west and east and south and north ;
      Awake and sing,
      Jesus is King,
All on this Christmas Day.

A Psalm of Gladness

My soul ! look up, rejoice and sing,
And to thy God oblations bring :
A ready will His will to learn,
A love that for His love will yearn,
A hunger for His righteousness,
A thirst for His abundant grace.

Lift up thy prayer to Him who hears,
And ask for freedom from thy fears ;
For faith that always will prevail,
For hope that nevermore can fail,
For joy of all He does for thee,
For peace with Him who makes thee free.

Lift up thy voice in gracious praise
And bless Him for His righteous ways ;
Exalt Him who created all,
And then redeemed thee from the fall,
And now makes clean thy heart within,
And saves it from the power of sin.

O let thy song grow sweeter still,
Since He thy nature came to fill
With graces pure and manifold,
More precious than all gifts of gold :
Who even was content to die
If so thou mightest reign on high.

Aye ! praise Him who vouchsafes to live
Within thee now, nor fails to give
Whatever thou can'st seek or need,
Who ceases not His death to plead
In thy behalf before the throne,
Nor ever leaves thee sad and lone.

O sing some new and purer song,
And tell His mercies all day long,
Whose pardon flows in boundless streams,
Whose recompense before thee gleams,
Who saves thee from the dread abyss,
And takes thee soon to endless bliss !

By Thy Cross and Passion

SAVIOUR, lifted on the tree !
Draw my spirit unto Thee :
Take away my heavy load,
Strengthen me to walk the road
That to light's great realm is leading,
Through the wounds that once were bleeding.

Jesus that wast crucified !
Keep me ever by Thy side ;
Make me know the truth divine,
Let it through my spirit shine :
Make me love the way of duty ;
Give me visions of Thy beauty.

For Thy dear and holy cross
Let me count all things but loss :
Cleanse my eyes to see how vain
Is this world of sin and pain :
Then upon the heavenly morrow
Turn to joy Thy servant's sorrow !

Why Weepest Thou?

WHY weepest thou? poor sorrower!
　　Whom seekest thou among these graves?
Thy Christ reveals Himself to thee
　　As one who by His rising saves.

Think not that Death can always hold
　　Thy treasures in his dreaded grasp,
Those blissful feet that walk in light
　　Thou shalt with joy undying clasp.

Dost thou not know that Jesus stands
　　Before the gate of every tomb,
To give to Faith this answer sweet,
　　That deep in heaven is yet more room?

That angels sit in sepulchres
　　Clothed in their garments of the light,
To watch while faithful ones lie still,
　　Wrapt in soft slumber of the night?

Then go and tell the news to all
　　That weep the weary hours away,
And trust His coming, soon or late,
　　To open wide the realms of day.

Easter

AWAKE and sing, ye dwellers in the dust,
For lo! the resurrection of the just!
Arise and shine, your lasting light is come,
Soar upward to your pure and saintly home.

Awake and sing, immortal hearts of fire,
That now for visions of the King aspire;
Ye shall behold Him in His robes of light;
Rejoice, rejoice, He passeth into sight.

O never have ye known what vision is!
O never have ye felt so deep a bliss!
The end for which He made you now is won,
Behold the planets hasten to their Sun.

O now ye put on joy as night the day,
And leap with praises, that once knelt to pray:
Ye waken all the kingdoms of the light
To new and yet more holy anthems bright.

O fruitful voice of God! the mighty King:
O faithful power of Christ! Let everything
That breathes and loves and sweetly sings adore
The love that lives and sings for evermore!

It is the Lord

RISE up, my fair one, come away,
And clothe Thee with the golden day :
Forget the past, and let me be
Thy light and joy eternally.

Behold the vision in the skies !
The realms of beauty greet Thine eyes ;
See'st not afar that radiant dome ?
There is Thine everlasting home.

There will I all my glory show,
And all my saints shall love me so :
I never told them half the things
With whose bright fame all heaven rings.

Speed on, my fair one, haste away .
We need not linger by the way :
The future shines, the past is not,
Higher and higher is thy lot.

O blessed shalt Thou be, my dove,
My undefiled ! Thy Father's love
Shall compass Thee, and angels sweet
Shall gather to Thy shining feet.

And all that love Thee shall attend
The entrance of their holy friend :
And we shall find a glad new song
One blissful rapture to prolong !

Easter Joy

HAST thou seen the vision glorious ?
    Jesus is alive again :
Calm is He and all-victorious,
    Free from every grief and pain ;
Now the tomb a temple is,
Now the realms of death are His.

Hast thou heard the blessed story ?
    For believers heaven is won ;
Thou may'st dwell in endless glory
    With God's dear and only Son ;
Eden blossoms as of yore,
Life grows brighter evermore.

Hast thou felt the awful gladness?
    Thou art brother to thy King :
Far from earth and all its sadness
    Thou shalt soar on eagle's wing ;
For He is our risen Lord—
Jesus in our flesh adored.

Divine Gifts

A LIGHT shines out upon the sea,
Perchance some message comes towards thee
O who can tell what joys are sailing
To this dark shore where we sit wailing!

The love of God ordains us good
Long ere it can be understood:
His angels now prepare the treasures,
With which at last to fill our measures.

The stars beneath whose beams we rest
Rolled into shape before the crest
Of wave leaped up, or surge of mountains,
Yet only late shined here like fountains.

Before we sinned the Saviour's love
Pleaded our pardon there above;
Before we touched the sacred chalice
He saved us from sin's scornful malice.

Peace broods upon the solemn wave,
Fit is the time a boon to crave:
This is my prayer that heavenly morrow
Be ours though here we now have sorrow.

Saturday Evening

THIS sun that sets in radiant calm
Shall rise to-morrow to the psalm
Of thousands upon thousands, where
Altars are spread with linen fair.

And ere he sets again he'll shine
On consecrated bread and wine,
And tears that gleam awhile unshed
In eyes that seem to see the dead.

Then shall the holy psalms be sung,
And prayer shall rise on trembling tongue,
And soul shall speak to soul of Him
Who comes His vine to prune and trim.

Be clean and ready, O my heart
In such dear praise to take thy part!
In such sweet notes to sing awhile,
And sit beneath the Father's smile.

A light shall rest on Sion's hill,
God's presence shall the temple fill;
A light shall shine within the breast
That humbly goes to Him for rest.

Through all the consecrated hours
Rest midst the bloom of heavenly flowers,
Walk by the banks of heavenly streams,
Kneel when the torch immortal gleams.

Perhaps some holy day at even,
When many prayers pass into heaven,
Thy God will send an angel wise
To bear thee into Paradise.

Perhaps to-morrow's eventide
Shall see thee with the Crucified ;
In lowliness confess thy sin,
And pray that thou may'st enter in.

Sunday Morning

TO-DAY Thy mercy shines
    In many an ancient fane,
Over the sea in distant lands,
    In mountain and in plain.

Where saints have slept their sleep
    Through ages long agone,
Under the arches dim and gray,
    Under the towers of stone.

Te Deum still is sung,
    And all the holy psalms ;
Hymns, like the oil on Aaron's head,
    Pour down their fragrant balms.

The Apostolic creed,
    All glorious as of old,
Passes on notes of majesty
    In through the gates of gold.

The sacred word is taught,
    And souls of holy fear
And love and benedictions filled,
    To God in Christ draw near.

The Eucharistic feast,
　　With simple, solemn rite,
Is given to God and given to man
　　With gladness infinite.

Through this new land of ours
　　The same sweet mercy streams,
Where temples rise all consecrate,
　　Fair as the angels' dreams.

The world in God is one,
　　One faith unites mankind
In golden bonds prepared in heaven,
　　All have one hope, one mind.

To-day I, too, must sing ;
　　Prepare, my soul, to meet
Thy God, thy Saviour and thy Friend,
　　And taste His mercy sweet.

Lift up thyself, my heart,
　　Put on thy robe of praise,
Adorn thyself, and oh ! be clean
　　To sing such holy lays !

Sunday Evening

In an old legend rare and quaint,
A sunbeam covered by a saint
Beneath her veil continued bright
Long after day had turned to night.

The beams that filled the world to-day
Fade not, though noon has passed away :
In hearts that thought to hold them fast
Some tender glory long will last.

For Christ the Sun of Righteousness
Adorns the Church with truth and grace,
And on this holiest day in seven
Prepares our souls to dwell in heaven.

As in the wind the waves grow white
Our souls grow pure when from the height
Of blissful heaven the Holy Ghost
Breathes on " the Sacramental host."

O blest the penitential tears
That welcome everlasting years !
O blest the vows renewed to-day
That speed us on our homeward way !

O blest the recompense bestowed
Instead of all sin's weary load!
O blest the love upon us poured
By Him whom all the world adored!

O blest the people everywhere
Who laid aside their earthly care!
O blest the hearts that found a place
Wherein to see their Father's face!

And blest art thou, my soul, to-night
That entered deeper into light!
O may we all grow holier thus,
His love be perfected in us!

Eventide

BREEZES soft and odorous
That lay in the breast of the rose
Fly about at evening's close
To enjoy the calm and deep repose,
And fan mine eyelids feverous,
And fit my restless spirit thus
For night and starry glows.

Children's voices generous,
That sound like the stroke of the spheres,
Swell o'er the fields like other years,
Which sorrowful memory often hears,
Like gladness toned to piteous
Soft gentle cries all-duteous,
No longer fraught with tears.

Blessings bland and beauteous,
That fill all the earth and the sky,
Float over me and make me sigh
For comfort and peace with God on high,
And voice of harp victorious,
And sight of Him all-glorious
In His felicity.

Be Not Silent Unto Me

JESUS ! let me hear Thee speak
    While the sunlight fades away,
While the stars in beauty break
    Through the gloom with crystal ray.

'Twas Thy wont at eventide
    With Thy mother to sit long,
Gazing at the heavens so wide,
    Breathing David's pastoral song.

Oft her gentle soul would droop
    With a strange and shadowy fear,
And Thy psalm would softly stoop
    On low wings to give her cheer.

Then as darkness deeper fell
    Rising higher Thy voice would bear
Messages to some sweet dell,
    When Thy kinsmen tarried there.

Jesus ! here I sit and long
    For some holy, tender word,
For some echo of the song
    That to-night in heaven is heard.

Be not silent unto me,
    Tell of mercy, hope and peace ;
I, Thy kinsman, wait on Thee
    For Thy merciful release.

Tell me of unfailing love,
    Tell me that my sin's forgiven,
Tell me, Thou that sit'st above,
    There is rest for me in heaven.

Jesus ! Now will I rejoice
    And lie down and take my rest,
For I hear Thy gracious voice,
    And who heareth it is blest.

Spread Thy mercy o'er the lands,
    Bless the weary, sick and poor,
Rest, O Lord, worn hearts and hands,
    Shed Thy light through every door.

A Little Hymn at Even

A GOLDEN light is in the West,
A heavenly hope is in my breast :
A few short hours and morn will come,
A little while and I go home.

O Father ! well I know the love
And mercy which I daily prove ;
Infinite love that comforts me,
A tender mercy, rich and free.

The countless stars shine clear and bright,
And make a temple of the night ;
Oh, from pure hearts may anthems rise
To Thee enthroned upon the skies !

Soft breezes blow from out the West,
Oh, may Thy Spirit bring me rest !
Sweet sounds arise from fields and streams,
May heavenly songs steal through my dreams.

The dews fall silent o'er the land,
Shed pardon gently from Thy hand;
The world seems fresh and calm and still,
Immortal God! my spirit fill.

Long time I gaze upon the stars,
Heaven seems to burst her ancient bars;
Ah, then! by faith I'll look to Thee
All night, and Thou'lt descend to me.

Glorying in Jesus

For righteousness I hunger and I thirst,
    Let me be filled with Thy sweet mercy, Lord ;
Before all things I seek Thy kingdom first,
    O let me find, according to Thy word.

With feeble hand I knock upon the door,
    Let it be opened soon lest I should faint;
With tears and groans Thy pity I implore,
    O listen to my sorrowful complaint.

I mourn the loss of many hopes and joys,
    Let me be comforted by Thy rich grace;
I tire of all earth's sordid dust and noise,
    Bring Thou my spirit to Thy hiding place.

O nothing have I done all worthily,
    No fruit have I to just perfection brought,
In all, in all but failure do I see,
    But I remember what my Saviour wrought.

Yes! I remember, and I turn to Thee,
    That never failest them that seek Thy face ;
With only mercy for my dying plea ;
    Jesus! I glory in Thy love and grace.

Spiritual Joys

LET me feed among the lilies,
    Let me rest beside the well,
Touch and taste the fruits so precious
    In the fields invisible.

Let me love the things eternal
    That appear when sight grows dim,
Glow with hopes of heavenly music,
    And the sweet undying hymn.

Even now the world all holy
    Breaks upon the vision clear,
God enthroned in rays of beauty
    Seems to draw so very near.

Like the shadow on the mountain
    From the cloud that passes by
Is His hand of peace and blessing
    Stretched athwart my heavenward eye.

Like the shadow on the fountain
    From the trees that wave above
Is the trembling of His presence
    On my trembling heart of love.

Thou art waiting to be gracious,
 For Thy mercy, Lord, I wait;
Blessed be the name victorious
 Which has opened wide the gate!

Blessed be that world of beauty
 And the festival of saints
Now prepared for souls repentant,
 For my lowly soul that faints!

My Portion

CHRIST is my spirit's light
At morn and noon and night;
My heart is fresh with dews of grace,
Shed from His dying face.

If I have any grief
In Him I find relief,
And when my soul takes up its psalm
He poureth richer balm.

And when my spirit weak
Turns toward the future bleak,
And fears dim phantoms of the tomb,
He scattereth the gloom.

Within His face so kind
All comforts do I find
Against that hour when forth I go
Beyond those scenes of woe.

All will be over soon,
The wintry afternoon
Wins golden sunbeams in the West,
And I eternal rest!

Where Dwellest Thou?

O Master mine, where dwellest Thou?
    Wilt bid me come and see?
I fain would be where Thou art now,
    And through eternity.

Long time I wandered sad and lone,
    Through paths of aimless toil,
Finding no answer to my moan,
    For wounds no healing oil.

Fainting I fall along the way
    I knew Thou passest by
On gracious errands every day,
    And so would hear my sigh.

I feel forsaken in the earth
    And long for endless rest;
I cannot bear their empty mirth,
    O take me to Thy nest!

For I am like a weary dove
    With broken, trembling wings:
Unless Thou stretch Thy arms of love
    To Whom my spirit clings,

I cannot reach the pleasant door
    Where Thy disciples are,
Nor greet the saints that evermore
    Thy daily bounties share.

My raiment is all soiled and torn,
    Unfit for Thy abode,
My visage is all marred and worn,
    With many a crushing load.

But I have heard of garment bright
    Laid up within Thy store,
And bread and wine and oil to light
    The brow and heart that's sore.

And I have heard that none who sought
    Have ever sought in vain,
Though nothing in their hands they brought
    To give to Thee again.

I feel Thy powerful arm uphold ;
    My senses fade away ;
But when I wake the realms of gold
    Shall shine in morning's ray !

The Shepherd's Voice
S. John 10 : 4

I KNOW His voice. It is the Shepherd's call.
    It is the Lord! I must arise and go:
He bids me follow Him and leave you all
    A little while. A stranger calls not so.

I knew I should not hear that voice in vain,
    There would be something in it rare and sweet,
From answering which my heart could not refrain,
    And follow which I must, with eager feet.

I knew if once He called my heart would leap
    As lightning from the east e'en to the west:
For when He calls, He putteth forth His sheep,
    To lead them to the shadows where they rest.

I knew He ne'er would leave me all alone—
    Though all alone for love of me He died—
But come Himself and roll away the stone,
    And make the path of His salvation wide.

For He has led and taught me all the years,
    And He has daily, hourly called me friend:
I knew the gladness would cast out the fears,
    For having loved, He loves unto the end.